Marx Joyce
Abbott Hardy Machiavelli Chesterton Cooper Emerson Austen
Defoe Melville Montaigne Haggard Hugo Grimm
Carroll Christie Maupassant Eliot
Stoker Wilde Byron Molière
Engels Schiller
Garnett Fitzgerald Hawthorne Smith Kafka
Goethe Einstein Dostoyevsky Hall
Cotton Kipling Doyle Willis
Baum Henry Nietzsche
Leslie Dumas Flaubert Turgenev Balzac
Stockton Vatsyayana Crane
Burroughs Verne
Curtis Tocqueville Gogol Vinci
Homer Widger Tolstoy Whitman Busch
Darwin Thoreau Twain Scott
Potter Zola Lawrence Plato Harte
Freud Dickens Burton Hesse
Kant Jowett Stevenson
Andersen Cervantes
London Descartes Voltaire
Poe Aristotle Wells Cooke
Hale James Hastings
Bunner Shakespeare Irving
Richter Chambers
Doré da Shaw Benedict Alcott
Dante Chekhov Wodehouse Pushkin
Swift Newton

 tredition®

tredition was established in 2006 by Sandra Latusseck and Soenke Schulz. Based in Hamburg, Germany, tredition offers publishing solutions to authors and publishing houses, combined with world-wide distribution of printed and digital book content. tredition is uniquely positioned to enable authors and publishing houses to create books on their own terms and without conventional manu-facturing risks.

For more information please visit: www.tredition.com

TREDITION CLASSICS

This book is part of the TREDITION CLASSICS series. The creators of this series are united by passion for literature and driven by the intention of making all public domain books available in printed format again - worldwide. Most TREDITION CLASSICS titles have been out of print and off the bookstore shelves for decades. At tredition we believe that a great book never goes out of style and that its value is eternal. Several mostly non-profit literature projects provide content to tredition. To support their good work, tredition donates a portion of the proceeds from each sold copy. As a reader of a TREDITION CLASSICS book, you support our mission to save many of the amazing works of world literature from oblivion. See all available books at www.tredition.com.

Project Gutenberg

The content for this book has been graciously provided by Project Gutenberg. Project Gutenberg is a non-profit organization founded by Michael Hart in 1971 at the University of Illinois. The mission of Project Gutenberg is simple: To encourage the creation and distribu-tion of eBooks. Project Gutenberg is the first and largest collection of public domain eBooks.

The Farmer's Boy A Rural Poem

Robert Bloomfield

Imprint

This book is part of TREDITION CLASSICS

Author: Robert Bloomfield
Cover design: Buchgut, Berlin – Germany

Publisher: tredition GmbH, Hamburg - Germany
ISBN: 978-3-8424-6683-8

www.tredition.com
www.tredition.de

TO THE AUTHOR OF THE FARMER'S BOY.

I.

If wealth, if honour, at command were mine,
  And every boast Ambition could desire,
The pompous Gifts, sweet Bard, I would resign
  For the aft Music of thy tuneful Lyre,

II.

Which speaks the soul awake to every charm
  That Nature open'd from thy humble cot:
Speaks powers chill Indigence could not disarm;
  Proof to Humanity's severest lot.

III.

Thou Friend to Nature, and of Man the Friend;
  Of every generous and benignant cause;
The accents of thy glowing worth, unfeign'd,
  Live in the cadence of each feeling pause.
Here thought, alternate, in the noble Plan
Admires the POET, and reveres the Man.

25 Aug. 1800.

PREFACE

Having the satisfaction of introducing to the Public this very pleasing and characteristic POEM, the FARMER'S BOY, I think it will be agreeable to preface it with a short Account of the manner in which it came into my hands: and, which will be much more interesting to every Reader, a little History of the Author, which has been communicated to me by his Brother, and which I shall very nearly transcribe as it lies before me.

In *November* last year [Footnote: This was written in 1799.] I receiv'd a MS. which I was requested to read, and to give my opinion of it. It had before been shewn to some persons in *London*: whose indifference toward it may probably be explain'd when it is consider'd that it came to their hands under no circumstances of adventitious recommendation. With some a person must be rich, or titled, or fashionable as a literary name, or at least fashionable in some respect, good or bad, before any thing which he can offer will be thought worthy of notice.

I had been a little accustom'd to the effect of prejudices: and I was determin'd to judge, in the only just and reasonable way, of the Work, by the Work itself.

At first I confess, seeing it divided into the four Seasons, I had to encounter a prepossession not very advantageous to any writer: that the Author was treading in a path already so admirably trod by THOMSON; and might be adding one more to an attempt already so often, but so injudiciously and unhappily made, of transmuting that noble Poem from Blank Verse into Rhime; ... from its own pure native Gold into an alloyed Metal of incomparably less splendor, permanence, and worth.

I had soon, however, the pleasure of finding myself reliev'd from that apprehension: and of discovering, that, although the delineation of RURAL SCENERY naturally branches itself into these divisions, there was little else except the General Qualities of a musical ear, flowing numbers, Feeling, Piety, poetic Imagery and Animation, a taste for the picturesque, a true sense of the natural and pathetic, force of thought, and liveliness of imagination, which were in common between Thomson and this Author. And these are qualities which whoever has the eye, the heart, the awakened and surrounding intellect, and the diviner sense of the Poet, which alone can deserve the name, must possess.

But, with these general Characters of true Poetry, "*The Farmer's Boy*" has, as I have said, a character of its own. It is discriminated as much as the circumstances and habits, and situation, and ideas consequently associated, which are so widely diverse in the two Authors, could make it different. Simplicity, sweetness, a natural tenderness, that *molle atque facetum* which HORACE celebrates in the Eclogues of VIRGIL, will be found to belong to it.

I intend some farther and more particular CRITICAL REMARKS on this charming Performance. But I now pass to the Account of the Author himself, as given me by his Brother:… a Man to whom also I was entirely a stranger:… but whose Candor, good Sense, and brotherly Affection, appear in this Narrative; and of the justness of whose Understanding, and the Goodness of his Heart, I have had many Proofs, in consequence of a correspondence with him on different occasions which have since arisen, when this had made me acquainted with him, and interested me in his behalf.

In writing to me, Mr. GEORGE BLOOMFIELD, who is a Shoemaker also, as his
Brother, and lives at BURY, thus expresses himself.

"As I spent five years with the Author, from the time he was thirteen years and a half old [Footnote: This by farther recollection has since been discover'd and stated by Mr. G. and Mr. R. BLOOMFIELD not to be quite exact. See p. viii. C. L.] till he was turned of eighteen, the most interesting time of life (I mean the time that instruction is acquir'd, if acquir'd at all), I think I am able to give a better account of him than any one can, or than he can of himself: for his Modesty would not let him speak of his Temper, Disposition, or Morals."

"ROBERT was the younger Child of GEORGE BLOOMFIELD, a *Taylor*, at HONINGTON. [Footnote: This Village is between *Euston* and *Troston*, and about eight miles N E. of *Bury*. L.] His Father died when he was an infant under a year old. [Footnote: Our Author was born, as his Mother has obligingly informed me, 3 *Dec.* 1766. L.] His Mother [Footnote: ELIZABETH, Daughter of ROBERT MANBY. Vide Note at the end of this Preface.] was a Schoolmistress, and instructed her own Children with the others. He thus learn'd to read as soon as he learn'd to speak."

"Though the Mother was left a Widow with six small Children, yet with the help of Friends she manag'd to give each of them a little schooling."

"ROBERT was accordingly sent to Mr. RODWELL, [Footnote: This respectable Man is senior Clerk to the Magistrates of the Hundred of BLACKBOURN, in which Honington is situated, and has conducted himself with great propriety in this and other public employments. L.] of Ixworth, to be improved in *Writing*: but he did not go to that School more than two or three months, nor was ever sent to any other; his Mother again marrying when ROBERT was about seven years old."

"By her second Husband, JOHN GLOVER, she had another Family."

"When *Robert* was not above *eleven* years old, the late Mr. W. AUSTIN, of SAPISTON, [Footnote: This little Village adjoins to HONINGTON. L.] took him. And though it is customary for Farmers to pay such Boys only 1s. 6d. per week, yet he generously took him into the house. This reliev'd his Mother of any other expence than only of finding him a few things to wear: and this was more than she well knew how to do."

"She wrote therefore," Mr. G. BLOOMFIELD continues, "to me and my Brother NAT (then in London), to assist her; mentioning that he, ROBERT, was so small of his age that Mr. AUSTIN said he was not likely to be able to get his living by hard labour."

Mr. G. BLOOMFIELD on this inform'd his Mother that, if she would let him take the Boy with him, he would take him, and teach him to make shoes: and NAT promis'd to clothe him. The Mother, upon this offer, took coach and came to LONDON, to Mr. G.

BLOOMFIELD, with the Boy: for she said, she never should have been happy if she had not put him herself into his hands.

"She charg'd me," he adds, "*as I valued a Mothers Blessing, to watch over him, to set good Examples for him, and never to forget that he had lost his Father*." I religiously confine myself to Mr. G. BLOOMFIELD'S own words; and think I should wrong all the parties concern'd if in mentioning this pathetic and successful Admonition, I were to use any other. He came from Mr. AUSTIN'S 29 *June* 1781. [Footnote: This date of his coming to Town is added by Mr. BLOOMFIELD himself since the first Edition.]

Mr. G. BLOOMFIELD then lived at Mr. *Simm's*, No. 7, *Pitcher's-court, Bell-alley, Coleman-street*. "It is customary," he continues, "in such houses as are let to poor people in *London*, to have light Garrets fit for Mechanics to work in. In the Garret, where we had two turn-up Beds, and five of us worked, I received little ROBERT."

"As we were all single Men, Lodgers at a Shilling per week each, oar beds were coarse, and all things far from being clean and snug, like what *Robert* had left at SAPISTON. *Robert* was our man, to fetch all things to hand. At Noon he fetch'd our Dinners from the Cook's Shop: and any one of our fellow workmen that wanted to have any thing fetched in, would send him, and assist in his work and teach him, for a recompense for his trouble."

"Every day when the Boy from the Public-house came for the pewter pots, and to hear what Porter was wanted, he always brought the yesterday's *Newspaper*. [Footnote: There was then, neither as a resource for the exigencies of finance, nor as a Principle of supposed Policy, that unhappy Check which prevails now on the circulation of *Newspapers*, and other means of *popular* Information. L.] The *reading* of the Paper we had been us'd to take by turns; but after *Robert* came, he mostly read for us,… because his time was of least value."

"He frequently met with words that he was unacquainted with: of this he often complain'd. I one day happen'd at a Book-stall to see a small Dictionary, which had been very ill us'd. I bought it for him for 4d. By the help of this he in little time could read and comprehend the long and beautiful speeches of BURKE, FOX, or NORTH.

"One Sunday, after an whole day's stroll in the country, we by accident went into a dissenting *Meeting-house* in the *Old Jewry*, where a Gentleman was lecturing. This Man fill'd *Robert* with astonishment. The House was amazingly crowded with the most genteel people; and though we were forc'd to stand still in the aisle, and were much press'd, yet *Robert* always quicken'd his steps to get into the Town on a Sunday evening soon enough to attend this Lecture.

"The Preacher lived somewhere at the West End of the Town ... his name was
FAWCET. His language," says Mr. G. BLOOMFIELD, "was just such as the
Rambler is written in; his Action like a person acting a Tragedy; his Discourse rational, and free from the Cant of Methodism.

"Of him *Robert* learn'd to accent what he call'd *hard* words; and otherwise improv'd himself; and gain'd the most enlarg'd notions of PROVIDENCE.

"He went sometimes with me to a *Debating Society* [Footnote: It is another of the Constitutional Refinements of these times to have fetter'd, and as to every valuable purpose, silenc'd, these Debating Societies. They were at least, to say the lowest of them, far better amusements than drunkenness, gambling, or fighting. They were no useless Schools to some of our very celebrated Speakers at the Bar and in Parliament: and, what is of infinitely more importance, they contributed to the diffusion of Political Knowledge and Public Sentiment. L.] at *Coachmaker's-hall*, but not often; and a few times to *Covent-garden Theatre*. These are all the opportunities he ever had to learn from Public Speakers. As to *Books*, he had to wade through two or three Folios: an *History of England, British Traveller*, and a *Geography*. But he always read them as a task, or to oblige us who bought them. And as they came in sixpenny numbers weekly, he had about as many hours to read as other boys spend in play."

"I at that time," proceeds his Brother, "read the *London Magazine*; and in that work about two sheets were set apart for a *Review* ... *Robert* seem'd always eager to read this Review. Here he could see what the Literary Men were doing, and learn how to judge of the merits of the Works that came out. And I observ'd that he always looked at the *Poet's Corner*. And one day he repeated a *Song* which he compos'd to an old tune. I was much surpris'd that a boy of sixteen [Footnote: He was probably 17; as appears on the statement from the Author himself. See N. to p. xvii.] should make so smooth verses: so I persuaded him to try whether the Editor of our Paper would give them a place in *Poet's Corner*. And he succeeded, and they were printed. And as I forget his other early productions, I shall copy this."

THE MILK-MAID, ON THE FIRST OF MAY.

Hail, MAY! lovely MAY! how replenish'd my pails!
  The young Dawn overspreads the East streak'd with gold!
My glad heart beats time to the laugh of the Vales,
  And COLIN'S voice rings through the woods from the fold.

The Wood to the Mountain submissively bends,
  Whose blue misty summits first glow with the sun!
See thence a gay train by the wild rill descends
  To join the glad sports:… hark! the tumult's begun.

Be cloudless, ye skies!… Be my Colin but there,
  Not the dew-spangled bents on the wide level Dale,
Nor Morning's first blush can more lovely appear
  Than his looks, since my wishes I could not conceal.

Swift down the mad dance, while blest health prompts to move,
  We'll count joys to come, and exchange Vows of truth;
And haply when Age cools the transports of Love,
  Decry, like good folks, the vain pleasures of youth.

No, no; the remembrance shall ever be dear!
  At no time LOVE with INNOCENCE ceases to charm:
It is transport in Youth … and it smiles through the tear,
  When they feel, in their children, its first soft alarm.

   The Writer of this Preface doubts whether he has been successful
in adding the last Stanza to this beautiful and simply expressive
song. But he imagin'd that some thought of this kind was in the
mind of the Author: and he was willing to endeavour to express it.
The Breast which has felt Love, justly shrinks from the idea of its
total extinction, as from annihilation itself. And there is even an
high social and moral use in that order of Providence which exalts
Sensations into tender and benign Passions; those Passions into

habitual Affections yet more tender; and raises from those Affections *Virtues* the most permanent, the most necessary and beneficent, and the most endearing: thus expanding the sentiment into all the Charities of domestic and social Life.

"I remember," says Mr. G. BLOOMFIELD, continuing his Narrative, "a little piece which he called the Sailor's Return: [Footnote: It is much to be wished that this may be discovered. L.] in which he tried to describe the feelings of an honest *Tar*, who, after a long absence, saw his dear native Village first rising into view. This too obtain'd a place in the Poet's Corner."

"And as he was so young," his brother proceeds, "it shews some Genius in him, and some Industry, to have acquir'd so much knowledge of the use of words in so little time. Indeed at this time myself and my fellow workmen in the Garret began to get instructions from him, though not more than sixteen years old." [Footnote: What simple magnanimity and benevolence in this Remark. L.]

"About this time there came a Man to lodge at our Lodgings that was troubled with fits. ROBERT was so much hurt to see this poor creature drawn into such frightful forms, and to hear his horrid screams, that I was forced to leave the Lodging. We went to *Blue Hart-court, Bell-alley*. In our new Garret we found a singular character, *James Kay*, a native of *Dundee*. He was a middle-aged man, of a good understanding, and yet a furious *Calvinist*. He had many Books, ... and some which he did not value: such as the SEASONS, PARADISE LOST, and some *Novels*. These Books he lent to ROBERT; who spent all his leisure hours in reading the *Seasons*, which he was now capable of reading. I never heard him give so much praise to any Book as to that."

"I think it was in the year 1784 that the Question came to be decided between the *journeymen Shoemakers*; whether those who had learn'd without serving an *Apprenticeship* could follow the Trade."

[Footnote: That is *as journeymen*: for there was no question that they could not as *Masters* on their *own* account. That a person may work as a *journeyman* without having served an apprenticeship, had already been determined, T. 9. G. 3. *Beach v. Turner*. Burr. Mansf. 2449. A person also who has not served an Apprenticeship may be a partner, contributing money, or advice and attention to the accounts and general concerns of the Trade, provided that he does not actual-ly exercise the Trade, and that the acting partner has served. Vide *Reynolds* v. *Chase*, M. 30. G. 2. Burr. Mansf. 2. 1 Burn. J.P. Apprent. § 12. L.]

"The Man by whom *Robert* and I were employ'd, Mr. Chamber-layne, of *Cheapside*, took an active part against the lawful journey-men; and even went so far as to pay off every man that worked for him that had joined their Clubs. This so exasperated the men, that their acting Committee soon looked for *unlawful men* (as they called them) among *Chamberlayne's* workmen."

They found out little *Robert*, and threatened to prosecute *Chamler-layne* for employing him, and to prosecute his Brother, Mr. *G. Bloom-field*, for teaching him. Chamberlayne requested of the Brother to go on and bring it to a Trial; for that he would defend it; and that nei-ther *George* nor *Robert* should be hurt.

In the mean time *George* was much insulted for having refus'd to join upon this occasion those who call'd themselves, exclusively, the *Lawful Crafts. George*, who says he was never famed for patience, (it is not indeed so much as might be sometimes wish'd, very often the lot of strong and acute minds to possess largely of this virtue,) took his pen, and address'd a Letter to one of the most active of their Committee-men (a man of very bad character). In this, after stating that he took *Robert* at his Mother's request, he made free as well with the private character of this man as with the views of the Committee. "This," says *George*, "was very foolish; for it made things worse: but I felt too much to refrain."

What connects this episodical circumstance with the character of our
Author follows in his brother's words.

"*Robert* naturally fond of Peace, and fearful for my personal safe-ty, begg'd to be suffer'd to retire from the storm."

"He came home; and Mr. AUSTIN kindly bade him take his house for his home till he could return to me. And here, with his mind glowing with the fine Descriptions of rural scenery which he found in THOMSON'S SEASONS, he again retrac'd the very fields where first he began to think. Here, free from the smoke,[Footnote: But one word is altered in this Description; which reminds one of the *Omitte mirari beatae Fumum et opes* Strepitumque Romae. L.] the noise, the contention of the city, he imbibed that Love of rural Simplicity and rural Innocence, which fitted him, in a great degree, to be the writer of such a thing as the *Farmer's Boy*."

"Here he liv'd two Months:... at length, as the dispute in the trade still remain'd undecided, Mr. DUDBRIDGE offer'd to take *Robert* Apprentice, to secure him, at all events, from any consequences of the
Litigation."

He was bound by Mr. *Ingram*, of *Bell-alley*, to Mr. *John Dudbridge*. His Brother *George* paid five shillings for *Robert*, by way of form, as a premium. Dudbridge was their Landlord, and a *Freeman* of the *City* of *London*. He acted most honourably, and took no advantage of the power which the Indentures gave him. *George Bloomfield* staid with *Robert* till he found he could work as expertly as his self.

Mr. GEORGE BLOOMFIELD adds, "When I left London he was turned of eighteen; [Footnote: This should seem to require correction by setting the Age forward according to the Dates above stated. C.L.] and much of my happiness since has arisen from a constant correspondence which I have held with him."

"After I left him, he studied *Music*, and was a good player on the *Violin*."

"But as my Brother *Nat* had married a *Woolwich* woman, it happen'd that *Robert* took a fancy to MARY-ANNE CHURCH, a comely young woman of that town, whose Father is a boat-builder in the Government yard there. He married 12th Dec. 1790."[Footnote: This Date from the Author. C.L.] "Soon after he married, *Robert* told me, in a Letter, that 'he had sold his Fiddle and got a Wife.' Like most poor men, he got a wife first, and had to get household-stuff afterward. It took him some years to get out of ready furnished Lodgings. At length, by hard working, &c. he acquired a Bed of his own, and hired the room up one pair of stairs at 14, *Bell- alley*, *Coleman-street*. The Landlord kindly gave him leave to sit and work in the light *Garret*, two pair of stairs higher."

"In *this* Garret, amid six or seven other workmen, his active Mind employ'd itself in composing *the Farmer's Boy*."

"In my correspondence I have seen several *poetical* effusions of his; all of them of a good moral tendency; but which he very likely would think do him little credit: on that account I have not preserv'd them."

"ROBERT is a *Ladies Shoemaker*, and works for DAVIES, *Lombard-street*. He is of a slender make; of about 5 F. 4 I. high; very *dark* complexion…. His MOTHER, who is a very religions member of the *Church of England*, took all the pains she could in his infancy to make him pious: and as his Reason expanded, his love of God and Man increas'd with it. I never knew his fellow for mildness of temper and Goodness of Disposition. And since I left him, universally is he prais'd by those who know him best, for the best of Husbands, an indulgent Father, and quiet Neighbour. He is between thirty-three and four years old,[Footnote: Corrected from the above Date, p. vi, to his present Age, May 1800. C. L.] and has three Children;" two Daughters and a Son.[Footnote: Added from the information of Mr. R. BLOOMFIELD. *Hannah*, born 25 *Oct.* 1791. *Mary Anne*, 6 *Sept.* 1793. *Charles*, 15 *Sept.* 1798.]

Mr. GEORGE BLOOMFIELD concludes this clear, affectionate, and interesting Narrative, by a very kind Address to the Writer of this Preface. But, pleas'd as I am with the good opinion of a Man like him, I must not take praise to myself for not having neglected or suppress'd such a Work when it came into my hands. And I have no farther merit than that of seeing what it was impossible for an unprejudiced Mind not to see, and of doing what it was impossible not to do.

But I join with him cordially in his prayer, "that GOD, *the Giver of thought*, may, as mental light spreads, raise up many who will turn a listening ear, and will not despise

"The short and simple annals of the Poor."

Very few words will complete what remains to be added.

Struck with the Work, but not less struck with the remark, which is become a proverb, of the Roman Satirist, that "*it is not easy* [Footnote: Haud facile emergunt quorum virtutibus obstat Res angusta domi.] for those to emerge to notice whose circumstances obscure the observation of their Merits," I sent it to a Friend,[Footnote: This Friend, THOMAS HILL, Esq. I hope will forgive my mentioning him without asking his consent.] whom I knew to be above these prejudices: and who has deserv'd, and is deserving, well of the public, in many other instances, by his attention to Literature and the elegant Arts. He immediately express'd an high satisfaction in it; and communicated it to the Publishers. They adopted it upon terms honorable to themselves, and satisfactory to the Author, and to me in his behalf. They have publish'd it in a manner which speaks abundantly for itself; both as to the typographical accuracy and beauty, and the good taste and execution of the Ornaments in Wood.

My part has been this, and it has been a very pleasing one: to revise the MS. making occasionally corrections with respect to Orthography, and sometimes in the grammatical construction. The corrections, in point of Grammar, reduce themselves almost wholly to a circumstance of provincial usage, which even well educated persons in *Suffolk* and *Norfolk* do not wholly avoid; and which may be said, as to general custom, to have become in these Counties almost an established Dialect:... that of adopting the plural for the singular termination of verbs, so as to exclude the *s*. But not a line is added or substantially alter'd through the whole poem. I have requested the MS. to be preserv'd for the satisfaction of those who may wish to be satisfied on this head.

The *Proofs* have gone through my hands. It has been printed slowly: because most carefully: as it deserv'd to be printed.

I have no doubt of its Reception with the Public: I have none of its going down to Posterity with honor; which is not always the Fate of productions which are popular in their day.

Thus much I know:... that the Author, with a spirit amiable at all times, and which would have been rever'd by Antiquity, seems far less interested concerning any Fame or Advantage he may derive from it to himself, than in the pleasure of giving a printed Copy of it, as a tribute of duty and affection, to his MOTHER; in whose pleasure, if it succeeds, his filial heart places the gratification of which it is most desirous. It is much to be a POET, such as he will be found:... it is more to be such a MAN.

CAPEL LOFFT.

TROSTON, n. BURY, SUFFOLK.

12 Dec. 1799.

ELIZABETH MANBY, the Mother of the Author of this POEM, was sister to the wife of Mr. WILLIAM AUSTIN. I had written to Mr. GEORGE BLOOMFIELD to request the name, before Marriage, of his Mother. This gain'd me an Answer, which I have great pleasure in adding.

"The late Mr. AUSTIN'S wife was a Manby (my Mother's sister). And it may seem strange that, in the FARMER'S BOY, *Giles* no where calls him *Uncle*, but *Master*.... The treatment that my Brother *Robert* experienced from Mr. *Austin* did not differ in any respect from the treatment that all the Servant Boys experienc'd who lived with him. Mr. *Austin* was Father of fourteen Children by my Aunt (he never had any other wife). He left a decent provision for the five Children that surviv'd him: so that it could not be expected he should have any thing to give to poor Relations. And I don't see a possibility of making a difference between GILES and the Boys that were not related to Mr.*Austin*: for he treated all his Servants exactly as he did his Sons. They all work'd hard; all liv'd well. The DUKE had not a better Man Tenant to him than the late Mr. *Austin*. I saw numbers of the Husbandmen in tears when he was buried. He was beloved by all who knew him. But I imagine *Robert* thought that when he was speaking of Benevolence that was universal, he had no occasion to mention the accidental circumstance of his being related to the Good Man of whom he sung."

SUPPLEMENT

I have mention'd in the Preface "THE SAILOR'S RETURN", from an intimation by Mr. G. BLOOMFIELD. From the Author himself, Mr. ROBERT BLOOMFIELD, I am oblig'd with what part he can recollect of this SONG, which I was desirous to recover. It was written shortly after the PEACE with AMERICA and FRANCE. Probably some time in the *Spring* of 1784. The Author thinks the Title of it was "THE SOLDIER'S RETURN," and that it was occasion'd by the arrival of some Regiments of British Soldiers from remote parts of the Globe.

He says, "I have endeavour'd to bring it back to my mind: but can only remember the following; which is not the beginning nor the finish."

Round LYBIA'S south point, where from toils so late freed,
Sweet Hope cheer'd my soul as we clear'd the rough sea;
I strove midst the Tars to improve the ship's speed;
Nor thought I of aught but ANNA and THEE.

Here comes the dear Girl! comes with kind arms extended
To welcome me!… limbs numb'd with age fain would move.
My cheek feels the offspring of rapture warm blended,
With answering drops:… this the meed of chaste Love!

Rouse the Fire —

* * * * *

I think every Reader will be of opinion that it is indeed desirable the whole Song, of which this is a Fragment, should be recover'd. It will probably be found (according to the recollection of the Author) either in the *General Advertiser, Gazetteer,* or *Courant.* From these specimens, and some I have since had the pleasure to see in MS. Mr. BLOOMFIELD appears fully to possess the simple, yet elegant, pathetic, and animated flow of Composition, the sweetness of Diction, Thought, and Numbers, which the SONG or BALLAD in their best character require.

I now quote a little Fragment in *blank verse* from the same Letter: with a slight correction in a place or two where the distribution or mechanism of the lines was not exact.

SUBJECT. *An Harvest Scene: describing Gleaners return'd from the Field.*

—Welcome the Cot's
Warm walls!… thrice welcome Rest, by toil endear'd;
Each hard bed softening, healing every care.
Sleep on, ye gentle souls …
Unapprehensive of the midnight thief!
Or if bereft of all with pain acquir'd,
Your fall, with theirs compar'd who sink from affluence,
With hands unus'd to toil, and minds unus'd
To bend, how little felt! how soon repair'd!

The ear of the Author seems as sweetly attun'd to verse without as with Rhime: though his less practice has given him proportionally less exactness.

It reminds one of the simple, tender, and flowing melody of the blank verse of ROWE: or of some of the affecting passages in the *Paradise Regain'd* of MILTON.

Sweetness, pastoral Content, the innocent and benevolent heart *"with a little pleas'd,"* breathe indeed through the Poems, and in the manners and conversation, of the Author of THE FARMER'S BOY.

When the *Spirit* of CHRISTIANITY declares *"blessed are the meek,"* every heart which considers what meekness is, feels the truth of that blessedness. It may smooth the way, and prevent impediments, which a different temper raises to temporal felicity: it certainly assures that Heaven which is *within*: and is a pledge and anticipation of the Heaven hereafter.

It is pleasing to think on a remark of Mr. GEO. BLOOMFIELD concerning his Brother when he first went to LONDON. "I have him in my mind's eye a little Boy; not bigger than Boys generally are at twelve years old. When I met him and his Mother at the Inn, [Footnote: In Bishopsgate-street.] he strutted before us, dress'd just as he came from keeping Sheep, Hogs, &c…. his shoes fill'd full of stumps in the heels. He looking about him, slip'd up … his nails were unus'd to a flat pavement. I remember viewing him as he scamper'd up … how small he was. Little thought, that little fatherless Boy would be one day known and esteem'd by the most learned, the most respected, the wisest and the best men of the Kingdom."

The brotherly overflowing of the heart in this passage I felt when I read the Letter (dated 27 *March* last), and cannot deny to others the pleasure of feeling it.

And those who have shewn themselves the FRIENDS of the FARMER'S BOY must excuse me if I mention some of them whose liberal and zealous attention had excited those feelings in the heart of his Brother, and have fill'd his with sentiments of thankfulness. The Duke of GRAFTON has every way shewn himself attentive to the Genius, the Worth, of Mr. BLOOMFIELD. He has essentially added to his comforts. His R. H. the Duke of YORK, by Capt. BUN-BURY, has made a liberal present, as an acknowledgment of the pleasure receiv'd from the perusal of his excellent Poem. This attention of his R. H. liberal and amiable in itself, has been the cause of like liberality in others. It suggested to Dr. DRAKE, and other Gentlemen at HADLEIGH, the idea of a local subscription of a Guinea each in that Town and Neighbourhood. This has been carried into effect by himself and eleven other Friends, who may be said in this instance to sustain, in a manner, the honorable function of a kind of LITERARY JURY. The Names who have given this testimony of their high esteem to the character of Mr. BLOOMFIELD, and of the pleasure they have received from the perusal of his Poem, are:

THOMAS SHERLOCKE GOOCH, Esq.
Major POCKLINGTON,
Dr. GIBBONS, M.D.
The Rev. J. PLAMPIN,
The Rev. T. KNOTTESFORD,
The Rev. R. PRITCHETT,
ABRAHAM REEVE, Esq.
GEO. ARCHER, Esq.
J. MILLS, Esq.
Mrs. TRAIL,
Mrs. LEAKE,
NATHAN DRAKE, M.D.

I have transcribed the names in the order in which they were transmitted to me. With a large proportion of those who have thus stood forth the Friends of Genius and Worth I have the pleasure of being acquainted. It gives me much satisfaction to mention this notice: welcome to the Author as a Gift; and far more so as a testimony of good opinion unexpectedly offer'd. Several instances of similar attention to the disproportion between the circumstances of the Author and the excellence of his poetical Talents and moral Qualities have spontaneously manifested themselves from different quarters. Those, as the separate act of individuals, I have not particularized otherwise than by this general acknowledgment: though many such have been mention'd to me by the Author. This, as a collective act, I hope I may be allow'd the gratification of thus noticing.

Sir CHARLES BUNBURY has warmly expressed his approbation of the Poem; as not only excellent for a Farmer's Boy, but such as would do honour to any person, whatever his education: and he also has much contributed to make it early and advantageously known. Mr. GREEN of IPSWICH has spoken of it as a charming composition: reflecting, in a very natural and vivid manner, the series of interesting images which touch'd the sensibility of a young, an artless, but a most intelligent observer of Nature; plac'd in a situation highly favourable to observation, though in fact not often productive of it. That Originality in such a subject is invaluable: and that this Poem appears to him (I know few men so qualified to judge on such a point) throughout original. And literary characters who have earnt to themselves much of true Praise by their own Productions, Mr. DYER and Dr. DRAKE of HADLEIGH, have given full and appropriate encomium to the excellence both in Plan and Execution, of this admirable RURAL PORM. My Friend Mr. BLACK of *Woodbridge*, has notic'd it in a very pleasing and characteristic Letter address'd to me in verse. I believe I shall not be just to the FARMER's BOY if I omit to notice that the Taste and Genius of Mrs. OPIE, born to do honour to every department of the Fine Arts, have given her an high sentiment of its merits. And a LADY at BURY, whom I wish I were permitted to name, has most truly characteriz'd it by remarking, that "the descriptions of Country scenes, occupations, customs, and manners, are as natural as possible: and that the justness, virtue, and tenderness of the sentiments are to be equally admired." Were I to name all the Friends and Admirers of the POEM and of the simple and amiable manners and character of the

AUTHOR, I should name, I believe, nearly every person in this Island whom I respect, esteem, and admire.

It would be highly gratifying to me could I now transcribe those testimonies to which I have generally referr'd:… but I abstain here from this: and the rather, as I believe Mr. DYER will probably soon express, in a Publication of his own, his sentiments on this Work; and as Dr. DRAKE, I know, has been so struck with it as to intend to appropriate to an investigation of its peculiar merit the concluding part of an enlarg'd Edition of his LITERARY HOURS.[Footnote: This has been since excellently perform'd by him. See the APPEN-DIX.]

The mention already made of the FARMER'S BOY in the NEW LONDON REVIEW and in the MONTHLY MIRROR I have seen with pleasure. I rejoice in that Fame which is just to living Merit, and waits not for the Tomb to present the tardy and then unvalued Wreath: I rejoice in the sense express'd not only of his Genius, but of his pure, benevolent, amiable Virtue, his affectionate Veneration to the DEITY, and his good Will to all…. Obscurity and Adversity have not broken; Fame and Prosperity, I am persuaded, will not corrupt him.

I cannot deny myself the satisfaction of mentioning that, after an absence of twelve years, the Author of the Farmer's Boy has revisit-ed his native Plains. That he has seen his Mother in health and spir-its: seen her with a joy to both which even his own most expressive and pathetic language would imperfectly describe…. Seen other near, affectionate, and belov'd Relatives: review'd, with the feelings of a truly poetic and benevolent Mind, the haunts of his youth; the Woods and Vales, the Cot, the Field and the Tree, which even recol-lected after so many years and at a distance, had awaken'd in such a manner the energies of his Heart and Intellect, and had inspir'd strains which will never cease to be repeated with pleasure and admiration. That he has been receiv'd at BURY with an emulous desire of his society; and certainly with the greatest reason. I rejoice that I at length have been made personally acquainted with him: that I have seen him here, and at his Mother's, and at Bury: that I have discours'd with him; that we have made our rural walks to-gether: that I have heard him read some of those Poems which are not yet printed; but which when they shall be so, will support fully and extend the Fame he has acquir'd. Though I have spent, occasionally, much of my life among persons worthy of Admiration and of Esteem, I can recollect few days so interesting and so valuable to me as these.

C.L.

TROSTON, 25 May, 1800.

What I have said in prose, p. ix of this Preface, is charmingly expressed in the language of the Muses by Mr. COLLIER, in his Miscellaneous Poems lately publish'd.

O where on earth can he a pleasure find
  Whose heart th' extatic sweets of Love has known,
When in the jarring chaos of his mind
  The gentle God no longer holds his throne!

ON REVISITING THE PLACE OF MY NATIVITY.

Though Winter's frowns had damp'd the beaming eye,
Through Twelve successive Summers heav'd the sigh,
The unaccomplish'd wish was still the same;
Till May in new and sudden glories came!
My heart was rous'd; and Fancy on the wing,
Thus heard the language of enchanting Spring:—

'Come to thy native groves and fruitful fields!
Thou know'st the fragrance that the wild-flow'r yields;
Inhale the Breeze that bends the purple bud,
And plays along the margin of the Wood.
I've cloth'd them all; the very Woods where thou
In infancy learn'd'st praise from every bough.
Would'st thou behold again the vernal day?
My reign is short;—this instant come away:
Ere Philomel shall silent meet the morn;
She hails the green, but not the rip'ning corn.
Come, ere the pastures lose their yellow flow'rs:
Come now; with heart as jocund as the hours.'

Who could resist the call?—that, Giles had done,
Nor heard the Birds, nor seen the rising Sun;
Had not Benevolence, with cheering ray,
And Greatness stoop'd, indulgent to display
Praise which does surely not to Giles belong,
But to the objects that inspir'd his song.
Immediate pleasure from those praises flow'd:
Remoter bliss within his bosom glow'd!
Now tasted all:—for I have heard and seen
The long-remember'd voice, the church, the green;—
And oft by Friendship's gentle hand been led
Where many an hospitable board was spread.
These would I name,… but each, and all can feel

What the full heart would willingly reveal:
Nor needs be told; that at each season's birth,
Still the enamell'd, or the scorching Earth
Gave, as each morn or weary night would come,
Ideal sweetness to my distant home:—
Ideal now no more;—for, to my view
Spring's promise rose, how admirably true!!
The early chorus of the cheerful Grove,
Gave point to Gratitude; and fire to Love.
O Memory! shield me from the World's poor strife;
And give those scenes thine everlasting life!

ROB. BLOOMFIELD.

LONDON, MAY 30, 1800.

SPRING.

ARGUMENT.

Invocation, &c. Seed time. Harrowing. Morning walks. Milking. The Dairy. Suffolk Cheese. Spring coming forth. Sheep fond of changing. Lambs at play. The Butcher, &c.

[Illustration]

SPRING

I.

O come, blest Spirit! whatsoe'er thou art,
Thou rushing warmth that hover'st round my heart,
Sweet inmate, hail! thou source of sterling joy,
That poverty itself cannot destroy,
Be thou my Muse; and faithful still to me,
Retrace the paths of wild obscurity.
No deeds of arms my humble lines rehearse,
No *Alpine* wonders thunder through my verse,
The roaring cataract, the snow-topt hill,
Inspiring awe, till breath itself stands still:
Nature's sublimer scenes ne'er charm'd mine eyes,
Nor Science led me through the boundless skies;
From meaner objects far my raptures flow:
O point these raptures! bid my bosom glow!
And lead my soul to ecstasies of praise
For all the blessings of my infant days!
Bear me through regions where gay Fancy dwells;
But mould to Truth's fair form what Memory tells.

Live, trifling incidents, and grace my song,
That to the humblest menial belong:
To him whose drudgery unheeded goes,
His joys unreckon'd as his cares or woes;
Though joys and cares in every path are sown,
And youthful minds have feelings of their own,
Quick springing sorrows, transient as the dew,
Delights from trifles, trifles ever, new.
'Twas thus with GILES: meek, fatherless, and poor:
Labour his portion, but he felt no more;
No stripes, no tyranny his steps pursu'd;
His life was constant, cheerful, servitude:
Strange to the world, he wore a bashful look,

The fields his study, Nature was his book;
And, as revolving SEASONS chang'd the scene
From heat to cold, tempestuous to serene,
Though every change still varied his employ,
Yet each new duty brought its share of joy.

Where noble GRAFTON spreads his rich domains,
Round *Euston's* water'd vale, and sloping plains,
Where woods and groves in solemn grandeur rise,
Where the kite brooding unmolested flies;
The woodcock and the painted pheasant race,
And sculking foxes, destin'd for the chace;
There Giles, untaught and unrepining, stray'd
Thro' every copse, and grove, and winding glade;
There his first thoughts to Nature's charms inclin'd,
That stamps devotion on th' inquiring mind.
A little farm his generous Master till'd,
Who with peculiar grace his station fill'd;
By deeds of hospitality endear'd,
Serv'd from affection, for his worth rever'd;
A happy offspring blest his plenteous board,
His fields were fruitful, and his harm well stor'd,
And fourscore ewes he fed, a sturdy team,
And lowing kine that grazed beside the stream:
Unceasing industry he kept in view;
And never lack'd a job for Giles to do.

FLED now the sullen murmurs of the North,
The splendid raiment of the SPRING peeps forth;
Her universal green, and the clear sky,
Delight still more and more the gazing eye.
Wide o'er the fields, in rising moisture strong,
Shoots up the simple flower, or creeps along
The mellow'd soil; imbibing fairer hues
Or sweets from frequent showers and evening dews;
That summon from its shed the slumb'ring ploughs,
While health impregnates every breeze that blows.
No wheels support the diving pointed share;

No groaning ox is doom'd to labour there;
No helpmates teach the docile steed his road;
(Alike unknown the plow-boy and the goad;)
But, unassisted through each toilsome day,
With smiling brow the plowman cleaves his way,
Draws his fresh parallels, and wid'ning still,
Treads slow the heavy dale, or climbs the hill:
Strong on the wing his busy followers play,
Where writhing earth-worms meet th' unwelcome day;
Till all is chang'd, and hill and level down
Assume a livery of sober brown:
Again disturb'd, when Giles with wearying strides
From ridge to ridge the ponderous harrow guides;
His heels deep sinking every step he goes,
Till dirt usurp the empire of his shoes.
Welcome green headland! firm beneath his feet;
Welcome the friendly bank's refreshing seat;
There, warm with toil, his panting horses browse
Their shelt'ring canopy of pendent boughs;
Till rest, delicious, chase each transient pain,
And new-born vigour swell in every vein.
Hour after hour, and day to day succeeds;
Till every clod and deep-drawn furrow spreads
To crumbling mould; a level surface clear,
And strew'd with corn to crown the rising year;
And o'er the whole Giles once transverse again,
In earth's moist bosom buries up the grain.
The work is done; no more to man is given;
The grateful farmer trusts the rest to Heaven.
Yet oft with anxious heart he looks around,
And marks the first green blade that breaks the ground;

[Illustration: a gate]

In fancy sees his trembling oats uprun,
His tufted barley yellow with the sun;
Sees clouds propitious shed their timely store,
And all his harvest gather'd round his door.
But still unsafe the big swoln grain below,

A fav'rite morsel with the Rook and Crow;
From field to field the flock increasing goes;
To level crops most formidable foes:
Their danger well the wary plunderers know,
And place a watch on some conspicuous bough;
Yet oft the sculking gunner by surprise
Will scatter death amongst them as they rise.
These, hung in triumph round the spacious field,
At best will but a short-lived terror yield:
Nor guards of property; (not penal law,
But harmless riflemen of rags and straw);
Familiariz'd to these, they boldly rove,
Nor heed such centinels that never move.
Let then your birds lie prostrate on the earth,
In dying posture, and with wings stretch'd forth;
Shift them at eve or morn from place to place,
And death shall terrify the pilfering race;
In the mid air, while circling round and round,
They call their lifeless comrades from the ground;
With quick'ning wing, and notes of loud alarm,
Warn the whole flock to shun the' impending harm.

This task had *Giles*, in fields remote from home:
Oft has he wish'd the rosy morn to come.
Yet never fam'd was he nor foremost found
To break the seal of sleep; his sleep was sound:
But when at day-break summon'd from his bed,
Light as the lark that carol'd o'er his head,
His sandy way deep-worn by hasty showers,
O'er-arch'd with oaks that form'd fantastic bow'rs,
Waving aloft their tow'ring branches proud,
In borrow'd tinges from the eastern cloud,
(Whence inspiration, pure as ever flow'd,
And genuine transport in his bosom glow'd)
His own shrill matin join'd the various notes
Of Nature's music, from a thousand throats:
The blackbird strove with emulation sweet,
And Echo answer'd from her close retreat;

The sporting white-throat on some twig's end borne,
Pour'd hymns to freedom and the rising morn;
Stopt in her song perchance the starting thrush
Shook a white shower from the black-thorn bush,
Where dew-drops thick as early blossoms hung,
And trembled as the minstrel sweetly sung.
Across his path, in either grove to hide,
The timid rabbit scouted by his side;
Or bold cock-pheasant stalk'd along the road,
Whose gold and purple tints alternate glow'd.
But groves no farther fenc'd the devious way;
A wide-extended heath before him lay,
Where on the grass the stagnant shower had run,
And shone a mirror to the rising sun,
(Thus doubly seen) lighting a distant wood,
Giving new life to each expanding bud;
Effacing quick the dewy foot-marks found,
Where prowling Reynard trod his nightly round;
To shun whose thefts 'twas Giles's evening care,
His feather'd victims to suspend in air,
High on the bough that nodded o'er his head,
And thus each morn to strew the field with dead.

His simple errand done, he homeward hies;
Another instantly its place supplies.
The clatt'ring dairy-maid immers'd in steam,
Singing and scrubbing midst her milk and cream,
Bawls out, *"Go fetch the cows:…"* he hears no more;
For pigs, and ducks, and turkies, throng the door,
And sitting hens, for constant war prepar'd;
A concert strange to that which late he heard.
Straight to the meadow then he whistling goes;
With well-known halloo calls his lazy cows:
Down the rich pasture heedlessly they graze,
Or hear the summon with an idle gaze;
For well they know the cow-yard yields no more
Its tempting fragrance, nor its wint'ry store.
Reluctance marks their steps, sedate and slow;

The right of conquest all the law they know:
Subordinate they one by one succeed;
And one among them always takes the lead,
Is ever foremost, wheresoe'er they stray;
Allow'd precedence, undisputed sway;
With jealous pride her station is maintain'd,
For many a broil that post of honour gain'd.
At home, the yard affords a grateful scene;
For Spring makes e'en a miry cow-yard clean.
Thence from its chalky bed behold convey'd
The rich manure that drenching winter made,
Which pil'd near home, grows green with many a weed,
A promis'd nutriment for Autumn's seed.
Forth comes the Maid, and like the morning smiles;
The Mistress too, and follow'd close by Giles.
A friendly tripod forms their humble seat,
With pails bright scour'd, and delicately sweet.
Where shadowing elms obstruct the morning ray,
Begins their work, begins the simple lay;
The full-charg'd udder yields its willing streams,
While *Mary* sings some lover's amorous dreams;
And crouching Giles beneath a neighbouring tree
Tugs o'er his pail, and chants with equal glee;
Whose hat with tatter'd brim, of nap so bare,
From the cow's side purloins a coat of hair,
A mottled ensign of his harmless trade,
An unambitious, peaceable cockade.
As unambitious too that cheerful aid
The mistress yields beside her rosy maid;

[Illustration: maid with a cow]

With joy she views her plenteous reeking store,
And bears a brimmer to the dairy door;
Her cows dismiss'd, the luscious mead to roam,
Till ere again recall them loaded home.
And now the DAIRY claims her choicest care,
And half her household find employment there:
Slow rolls the churn, its load of clogging cream

At once foregoes its quality and name;
From knotty particles first floating wide
Congealing butter's dash'd from side to side;
Streams of new milk thro' flowing coolers stray,
And snow-white curd abounds, and wholesome whey.
Due north th' unglazed windows, cold and clear,
For warming sunbeams are unwelcome here.
Brisk goes the work beneath each busy hand,
And *Giles* must trudge, whoever gives command;
A *Gibeonite*, that serves them all by turns:
He drains the pump, from him the faggot burns;
From him the noisy hogs demand their food;
While at his heels run many a chirping brood,
Or down his path in expectation stand,
With equal claims upon his strewing hand.
Thus wastes the morn, till each with pleasure sees
The bustle o'er, and press'd the new-made cheese.

Unrivall'd stands thy country CHEESE, O *Giles!*
Whose very name alone engenders smiles;
Whose fame abroad by every tongue is spoke,
The well-known butt of many a flinty joke,
That pass like current coin the nation through;
And, ah! experience proves the satire true.
Provision's grave, thou ever craving mart,
Dependant, huge Metropolis! where Art
Her pouring thousands stows in breathless rooms,
Midst pois'nous smokes and steams, and rattling looms;
Where Grandeur revels in unbounded stores;
Restraint, a slighted stranger at their doors!

[Illustration: man pouring feed into a trough]

Thou, like a whirlpool, drain'st the countries round,
Till London market, London price, resound
Through every town, round every passing load,
And dairy produce throngs the eastern road:
Delicious veal, and butter, every hour,

From Essex lowlands, and the banks of Stour;
And further far, where numerous herds repose,
From Orwell's brink, from Weveny, or Ouse.
Hence Suffolk dairy-wives run mad for cream,
And leave their milk with nothing but its name;
Its name derision and reproach pursue,
And strangers tell of "three times skimm'd sky-blue."
To cheese converted, what can be its boast?
What, but the common virtues of a post!
If drought o'ertake it faster than the knife,
Most fair it bids for stubborn length of life,
And, like the oaken shelf whereon 'tis laid,
Mocks the weak efforts of the bending blade;
Or in the hog-trough rests in perfect spite,
Too big to swallow, and too hard to bite.
Inglorious victory! Ye Cheshire meads,
Or Severn's flow'ry dales, where plenty treads,
Was your rich milk to suffer wrongs like these,
Farewell your pride! farewell renowned cheese!
The skimmer dread, whose ravages alone
Thus turn the mead's sweet nectar into stone.

NEGLECTED now the early *daisy* lies:
Nor thou, pale *primrose*, bloom'st the only prize:
Advancing SPRING profusely spreads abroad
Flow'rs of all hues, with sweetest fragrance stor'd;
Where'er she treads, LOVE gladdens every plain,
Delight on tiptoe bears her lucid train;
Sweet *Hope* with conscious brow before her flies,
Anticipating wealth from Summer skies;
All Nature feels her renovating sway;
The sheep-fed pasture, and the meadow gay;
And trees, and shrubs, no longer budding seen,
Display the new-grown branch of lighter green;
On airy downs the shepherd idling lies,
And sees to-morrow in the marbled skies.
Here then, my soul, thy darling theme pursue,

For every day was Giles a SHEPHERD too.

Small was his charge: no wilds had they to roam;
But bright enclosures circling round their home.
Nor yellow-blossom'd furze, nor stubborn thorn,
The heath's rough produce, had their fleeces torn:
Yet ever roving, ever seeking thee,
Enchanting spirit, dear Variety!
O happy tenants, prisoners of a day!
Releas'd to ease, to pleasure, and to play;
Indulg'd through every field by turns to range,
And taste them all in one continual change.
For though luxuriant their grassy food,
Sheep long confin'd but loathe the present good;
Bleating around the homeward gate they meet,
And starve, and pine, with plenty at their feet.
Loos'd from the winding lane, a joyful throng,
See, o'er yon pasture how they pour along!
Giles round their boundaries takes his usual stroll;
Sees every pass secur'd, and fences whole;
High fences, proud to charm the gazing eye,
Where many a nestling first assays to fly;
Where blows the woodbine, faintly streak'd with red,
And rests on every bough its tender head;
Round the young ash its twining branches meet,
Or crown the hawthorn with its odours sweet.

Say, ye that know, ye who have felt and seen,
Spring's morning smiles, and soul-enliv'ning green,
Say, did you give the thrilling transport way?
Did your eye brighten, when young lambs at play
Leap'd o'er your path with animated pride,
Or gaz'd in merry clusters by your side?
Ye who can smile, to wisdom no disgrace,
At the arch meaning of a kitten's face;
If spotless innocence, and infant mirth,
Excites to praise, or gives reflection birth;
In shades like these pursue your fav'rite joy,

Midst Nature's revels, sports that never cloy.

A few begin a short but vigorous race,
And indolence abash'd soon flies the place;
Thus challeng'd forth, see thither one by one,
From every side assembling playmates run;
A thousand wily antics mark their stay,
A starting crowd, impatient of delay.
Like the fond dove from fearful prison freed,
Each seems to say, "Come, let us try our speed;"
Away they scour, impetuous, ardent, strong,
The green turf trembling as they bound along;
Adown the slope, then up the hillock climb,
Where every molehill is a bed of thyme;
There panting stop; yet scarcely can refrain;
A bird, a leaf, will set them off again:
Or, if a gale with strength unusual blow,
Scatt'ring the wild-briar roses into snow,
Their little limbs increasing efforts try,
Like the torn flower the fair assemblage fly.
Ah, fallen rose! sad emblem of their doom;
Frail as thyself, they perish while they bloom!
Though unoffending innocence may plead,
Though frantic ewes may mourn the savage deed,
Their shepherd comes, a messenger of blood,
And drives them bleating from their sports and food.
Care loads his brow, and pity wrings his heart,
For lo, the murd'ring BUTCHER with his cart
Demands the firstlings of his flock to die,
And makes a sport of life and liberty!
His gay companions *Giles* beholds no more;
Clos'd are their eyes, their fleeces drench'd in gore;
Nor can Compassion, with her softest notes,
Withhold the knife that plunges through their throats.

Down, indignation! hence, ideas foul!
Away the shocking image from my soul!
Let kindlier visitants attend my way,

Beneath approaching *Summer's* fervid ray;
Nor thankless glooms obtrude, nor cares annoy,
Whilst the sweet theme is *universal joy.*

SUMMER.

ARGUMENT.

Turnip sowing. Wheat ripening. Sparrows. Insects. The sky-lark. Reaping, &c. Harvest-field, Dairy-maid, &c. Labours of the barn. The gander. Night; a thunder storm. Harvest-home. Reflections, &c.

[Illustration]

SUMMER.

THE FARMER'S life displays in every part
A moral lesson to the sensual heart.
Though in the lap of Plenty, thoughtful still,
He looks beyond the present good or ill;
Nor estimates alone one blessing's worth,
From changeful seasons, or capricious earth;
But views the future with the present hours,
And looks for failures as he looks for show'ers;
For casual as for certain want prepares,
And round his yard the reeking haystack rears;
Or clover, blossom'd lovely to the sight,
His team's rich store through many a wint'ry night.
What tho' abundance round his dwelling spreads,
Though ever moist his self-improving meads
Supply his dairy with a copious flood,
And seem to promise unexhausted food;
That promise fails, when buried deep in snow,
And vegetative juices cease to flow.
For this, his plough turns up the destin'd lands,
Whence stormy Winter draws its full demands;
For this, the seed minutely small he sows,
Whence, sound and sweet, the hardy turnip grows.
But how unlike to APRIL'S closing days!
High climbs the Sun, and darts his pow'rful rays;
Whitens the fresh-drawn mould, and pierces through
The cumb'rous clods that tumble round the plough.
O'er heaven's bright azure hence with joyful eyes
The Farmer sees dark clouds assembling rise;
Borne o'er his fields a heavy torrent falls,
And strikes the earth in hasty driving squalls.
"Right welcome down, ye precious drops," he cries;
But soon, too soon, the partial blessing flies.
"Boy, bring thy harrows, try how deep the rain

Has forc'd its way." He comes, but comes in vain;
Dry dust beneath the bubbling surface lurks,
And mocks his pains the more, the more he works:
Still midst huge clods he plunges on forlorn,
That laugh his harrows and the shower to scorn.
E'en thus the living clod, the stubborn fool,
Resists the stormy lectures of the school,
Till tried with gentler means, the dunce to please,
His head imbibes right reason by degrees;
As when from eve till morning's wakeful hour,
Light, constant rain, evinces secret pow'r,
And ere the day resume its wonted smiles,
Presents a cheerful easy task for *Giles*.
Down with a touch the mellow'd soil is laid,
And yon tall crop next claims his timely aid;
Thither well pleas'd he hies, assur'd to find
Wild trackless haunts, and objects to his mind.

Shot up from broad rank blades that droop below,
The nodding WHEAT-EAR forms a graceful bow,
With milky kernels starting full, weigh'd down,
Ere yet the sun hath ting'd its head with brown;
Whilst thousands in a flock, for ever gay,
Loud chirping *sparrows* welcome on the day,
And from the mazes of the leafy thorn
Drop one by one upon the bending corn.
Giles with a pole assails their close retreats,
And round the grass-grown dewy border beats,
On either side completely overspread,
Here branches bend, there corn o'ertops his head.
Green covert, hail! for through the varying year
No hours so sweet, no scene to him so dear.

[Illustration]

Here *Wisdom's* placid eye delighted sees
His frequent intervals of lonely ease,
And with one ray his infant soul inspires,

Just kindling there her never-dying fires,
Whence solitude derives peculiar charms,
And heaven-directed thought his bosom warms.
Just where the parting bough's light shadows play,
Scarce in the shade, nor in the scorching day,
Stretch'd on the turf he lies, a peopled bed,
Where swarming insects creep around his head.
The small dust-colour'd beetle climbs with pain
O'er the smooth plantain-leaf, a spacious plain!
Thence higher still, by countless steps convey'd,
He gains the summit of a shiv'ring blade,
And flirts his filmy wings, and looks around,
Exulting in his distance from the ground.
The tender speckled moth here dancing seen,
The vaulting grasshopper of glossy green,
And all prolific *Summer's* sporting train,
Their little lives by various pow'rs sustain.
But what can unassisted vision do?
What, but recoil where most it would pursue;
His patient gaze but finish with a sigh,
When musing waking speaks the *sky-lark* nigh!
Just starting from the corn she cheerly sings,
And trusts with conscious pride her downy wings;
Still louder breathes, and in the face of day
Mounts up, and calls on *Giles* to mark her way.
Close to his eyes his hat he instant bends,
And forms a friendly telescope, that lends
Just aid enough to dull the glaring light,
And place the wand'ring bird before his sight;
Yet oft beneath a cloud she sweeps along,
Lost for awhile, yet pours her varied song:
He views the spot, and as the cloud moves by,
Again she stretches up the clear blue sky;

[Illustration]

Her form, her motion, undistinguish'd quite,
Save when she wheels direct from shade to light:
The flutt'ring songstress a mere speck became,

Like fancy's floating bubbles in a dream;
He sees her yet, but yielding to repose,
Unwittingly his jaded eyelids close.
Delicious sleep! From sleep who could forbear,
With no more guilt than *Giles*, and no more care?
Peace o'er his slumbers waves her guardian wing,
Nor conscience once disturbs him with a sting;
He wakes refresh'd from every trivial pain,
And takes his pole and brushes round again.

Its dark-green hue, its sicklier tints all fail,
And rip'ening harvest rustles in the gale.
A glorious sight, if glory dwells below,
Where Heaven's munificence makes all the show,
O'er every field and golden prospect found,
That glads the ploughman's Sunday morning's round,
When on some eminence he takes his stand,
To judge the smiling produce of the land.
Here Vanity slinks back, her head to hide:
What is there here to flatter human pride?
The tow'ring fabric, or the dome's loud roar,
And stedfast columns, may astonish more,
Where the charm'd gazer long delighted stays,
Yet trac'd but to the *architect* the praise;
Whilst here, the veriest clown that treads the sod,
Without one scruple gives the praise to GOD;
And twofold joys possess his raptur'd mind,
From gratitude and admiration join'd.

Here, midst the boldest triumphs of her worth,
NATURE herself invites the REAPERS forth;
Dares the keen sickle from its twelvemonth's rest,
And gives that ardour which in every breast
From infancy to age alike appears,
When the first sheaf its plumy top uprears.

[Illustration]

No rake takes here what Heaven to all bestows—
Children of want, for you the bounty flows!
And every cottage from the plenteous store
Receives a burden nightly at its door.

Hark! where the sweeping scythe now rips along:
Each sturdy Mower emulous and strong;
Whose writhing form meridian heat defies,
Bends o'er his work, and every sinew tries;
Prostrates the waving treasure at his feet,
But spares the rising clover, short and sweet.
Come, HEALTH! come, *Jollity!* light-footed, come;
Here hold your revels, and make this your home.
Each heart awaits and hails you as its own;
Each moisten'd brow, that scorns to wear a frown:
Th' unpeopled dwelling mourns its tenants stray'd;
E'en the domestic laughing dairy maid
Hies to the FIELD, the general toil to share.
Meanwhile the FARMER quits his elbow-chair,
His cool brick-floor, his pitcher, and his ease,
And braves the sultry beams, and gladly sees
His gates thrown open, and his team abroad,
The ready group attendant on his word,
To turn the swarth, the quiv'ring load to rear,
Or ply the busy rake, the land to clear.
Summer's light garb itself now cumb'rous grown,
Each his thin doublet in the shade throws down;
Where oft the mastiff sculks with half-shut eye,
And rouses at the stranger passing by;
Whilst unrestrain'd the social converse flows,
And every breast Love's powerful impulse knows,
And rival wits with more than rustic grace
Confess the presence of a pretty face.

For, lo! encircled there, the lovely MAID,
In youth's own bloom and native smiles array'd;
Her hat awry, divested of her gown,

Her creaking stays of leather, stout and brown;…

[Illustration]

Invidious barrier! why art thou so high,
When the slight covering of her neck slips by,
There half revealing to the eager sight
Her full, ripe bosom, exquisitely white?
In many a local tale of harmless mirth,
And many a jest of momentary birth,
She bears a part, and as she stops to speak,
Strokes back the ringlets from her glowing cheek.

Now noon gone by, and four declining hours,
The weary limbs relax their boasted pow'rs;
Thirst rages strong, the fainting spirits fail,
And ask the sov'reign cordial, home-brew'd ale:
Beneath some shelt'ring heap of yellow corn
Rests the hoop'd keg, and friendly cooling horn,
That mocks alike the goblet's brittle frame,
Its costlier potions, and its nobler name.
To *Mary* first the brimming draught is given
By toil made welcome as the dews of heaven,
And never lip that press'd its homely edge
Had kinder blessings or a heartier pledge.

Of wholesome viands here a banquet smiles,
A common cheer for all;… e'en humble *Giles*,
Who joys his trivial services to yield
Amidst the fragrance of the open field;
Oft doom'd in suffocating heat to bear
The cobweb'd barn's impure and dusty air;
To ride in murky state the panting steed,
Destin'd aloft th' unloaded grain to tread,
Where, in his path as heaps on heaps are thrown,
He rears, and plunges the loose mountain down:
Laborious task! with what delight when done

Both horse and rider greet th' unclouded sun!

Yet by th' unclouded sun are hourly bred
The bold assailants that surround thine head,
Poor patient *Ball!* and with insulting wing
Roar in thine ears, and dart the piercing sting:
In thy behalf the crest-wav'd boughs avail
More than thy short-clipt remnant of a tail,
A moving mockery, a useless name,
A living proof of cruelty and shame.
Shame to the man, whatever fame he bore,
Who took from thee what man can ne'er restore,
Thy weapon of defence, thy chiefest good,
When swarming flies contending suck thy blood.
Nor thine alone the suff'ring, thine the care,
The fretful *Ewe* bemoans an equal share;
Tormented into sores, her head she hides,
Or angry brushes from her new-shorn sides.
Pen'd in the yard, e'en now at closing day
Unruly *Cows* with mark'd impatience stay,
And vainly striving to escape their foes,
The pail kick down; a piteous current flows.

Is't not enough that plagues like these molest?
Must still another foe annoy their rest?
He comes, the pest and terror of the yard,
His full-fledg'd progeny's imperious guard;
The GANDER;... spiteful, insolent, and bold,
At the colt's footlock takes his daring hold:
There, serpent-like, escapes a dreadful blow;
And straight attacks a poor defenceless cow:
Each booby goose th' unworthy strife enjoys,
And hails his prowess with redoubled noise.
Then back he stalks, of self-importance full,
Seizes the shaggy foretop of the bull,
Till whirl'd aloft he falls; a timely check,
Enough to dislocate his worthless neck:
For lo! of old, he boasts an honour'd wound;

Behold that broken wing that trails the ground!
Thus fools and bravoes kindred pranks pursue;
As savage quite, and oft as fatal too.
Happy the man that foils an envious elf,
Using the darts of spleen to serve himself.
As when by turns the strolling *Swine* engage
The utmost efforts of the bully's rage,
Whose nibbling warfare on the grunter's side
Is welcome pleasure to his oristly hide;
Gently he stoops, or strecht at ease along,
Enjoys the insults of the gabbling throng,
That march exulting round his fallen head,
As human victors trample on their dead.

Still TWILIGHT, welcome! Rest, how sweet art thou!
Now eve o'erhangs the western cloud's thick brow:
The far-stretch'd curtain of retiring light,
With fiery treasures fraught; that on the sight
Flash from its bulging sides, where darkness lours,
In Fancy's eye, a chain of mould'ring tow'rs;
Or craggy coasts just rising into view,
Midst jav'lins dire, and darts of streaming blue.

Anon tir'd labourers bless their shelt'ring home,
When MIDNIGHT, and the frightful TEMPEST come.
The Farmer wakes, and sees with silent dread
The angry shafts of Heaven gleam round his bed;
The bursting cloud reiterated roars,
Shakes his straw roof, and jars his bolted doors:
The slow-wing'd storm along the troubled skies
Spreads its dark course; the wind begins to rise;
And full-leaf'd elms, his dwelling's shade by day,
With mimic thunder give its fury way:
Sounds in his chimney top a doleful peal,
Midst pouring rain, or gusts of rattling hail;
With tenfold danger low the tempest bends,
And quick and strong the sulph'urous flame descends:
The fright'ned mastiff from his kennel flies,

And cringes at the door with piteous cries....

Where now's the trifler? where the child of pride?
These are the moments when the heart is try'd!
Nor lives the man with conscience e'er so clear,
But feels a solemn, reverential fear;
Feels too a joy relieve his aching breast,
When the spent storm hath howl'd itself to rest.
Still, welcome beats the long continued show'r,
And sleep protracted, comes with double pow'r;
Calm dreams of bliss bring on the morning sun,
For every barn is fill'd, and HARVEST *done*!

Now, ere sweet SUMMER bids its long adieu,
And winds blow keen where late the blossom grew,
The bustling day and jovial night must come,
The long accustom'd feast of HARVEST-HOME.
No blood-stain'd victory, in story bright,
Can give the philosophic mind delight;
No triumph please while rage and death destroy:
Reflection sickens at the monstrous joy.
And where the joy, if rightly understood,
Like cheerful praise for universal good?
The soul nor check nor doubtful anguish knows,
But free and pure the grateful current flows.

Behold the sound oak table's massy frame
Bestride the kitchen floor! the careful dame
And gen'rous host invite their friends around,
While all that clear'd the crop, or till'd the ground,
Are guests by right of custom:... old and young;
And many a neighbouring yeoman join the throng,
With artizans that lent their dext'rous aid,
When o'er each field the flaming sun-beams play'd,—

Yet Plenty reigns, and from her boundless hoard,
Though not one jelly trembles on the board,

Supplies the feast with all that sense can crave;
With all that made our great forefathers brave,
Ere the cloy'd palate countless flavours try'd,
And cooks had Nature's judgment set aside.
With thanks to Heaven, and tales of rustic lore,
The mansion echoes when the banquet's o'er;
A wider circle spreads, and smiles abound,
As quick the frothing horn performs its round;
Care's mortal foe; that sprightly joys imparts
To cheer the frame and elevate their hearts.
Here, fresh and brown, the hazel's produce lies
In tempting heaps, and peals of laughter rise,
And crackling Music, with the frequent *Song*,
Unheeded bear the midnight hour along.

Here once a year Distinction low'rs its crest,
The master, servant, and the merry guest,
Are equal all; and round the happy ring
The reaper's eyes exulting glances fling,
And, warm'd with gratitude, he quits his place,
With sun-burnt hands and ale-enliven'd face,
Refills the jug his honour'd host to tend,
To serve at once the master and the friend;
Proud thus to meet his smiles, to share his tale,
His nuts, his conversation, and his ale.

Such were the days, … of days long past I sing,
When Pride gave place to mirth without a sting;
Ere tyrant customs strength sufficient bore
To violate the feelings of the poor;
To leave them distanc'd in the mad'ning race,
Where'er Refinement shews its hated face:
Nor causeless hated;… 'tis the peasant's curse,
That hourly makes his wretched station worse;
Destroys life's intercourse; the social plan
That rank to rank cements, as man to man:
Wealth flows around him, fashion lordly reigns;

Yet poverty is his, and mental pains.

Methinks I hear the mourner thus impart
The stifled murmurs of his wounded heart:
'Whence comes this change, ungracious, irksome, cold?
'Whence the new grandeur that mine eyes behold?
'The wid'ning distance which I daily see,
'Has Wealth done this?… then wealth's a foe to me;
'Foe to our rights; that leaves a pow'rful few
'The paths of emulation to pursue:…
'For emulation stoops to us no more:
'The hope of humble industry is o'er;
'The blameless hope, the cheering sweet presage
'Of future comforts for declining age.
'Can my sons share from this paternal hand
'The profits with the labours of the land?
'No; tho' indulgent Heaven its blessing deigns,
'Where's the small farm to suit my scanty means?
'Content, the Poet sings, with us resides;
'In lonely cots like mine the damsel hides;
'And will he then in raptur'd visions tell
'That sweet Content with Want can ever dwell?
'A barley loaf, 'tis true, my table crowns,
'That fast diminishing in lusty rounds,
'Stops Nature's cravings; yet her sighs will flow
'From knowing this,… that once it was not so.
'Our annual feast, when Earth her plenty yields,
'When crown'd with boughs the last load quits the fields,
'The aspect still of ancient joy puts on;
'The aspect only, with the substance gone:
'The self-same Horn is still at our command,
'But serves none now but the plebeian hand:
'For *home-brew'd Ale*, neglected and debas'd,
'Is quite discarded from the realms of taste.
'Where unaffected Freedom charm'd the soul,
'The separate table and the costly bowl,
'Cool as the blast that checks the budding Spring,
'A mockery of gladness round them fling.

'For oft the Farmer, ere his heart approves,
'Yields up the custom which he dearly loves:
'Refinement forces on him like a tide;
'Bold innovations down its current ride,
'That bear no peace beneath their shewy dress,
'Nor add one tittle to his happiness.
'His guests selected; rank's punctilios known;
'What trouble waits upon a casual frown!
'Restraint's foul manacles his pleasures maim;
'Selected guests selected phrases claim:
'Nor reigns that joy when hand in hand they join
'That good old Master felt in shaking mine.
'HEAVEN bless his memory! bless his honour'd name!
'(The poor will speak his lasting worthy fame:)
'To souls fair-purpos'd strength and guidance give;
'In pity to us still let goodness live:
'Let labour have its due! my cot shall be
'From chilling want and guilty murmurs free:
'Let labour have its due;… then peace is mine,
'And never, never shall my heart repine.'

AUTUMN.

ARGUMENT.

Acorns. Hogs in the wood. Wheat-sowing. The Church. Village girls. The mad girl. The bird-boy's hut. Disappointments; reflections, &c. Euston-hall. Fox-hunting. Old Trouncer. Long nights. A welcome to Winter.

[Illustration]

AUTUMN.

III.

Again, the year's *decline*, midst storms and floods,
The thund'ring chase, the yellow fading woods,
Invite my song; that fain would boldly tell
Of upland coverts, and the echoing dell,
By turns resounding loud, at eve and morn
The swineherd's halloo, or the huntsman's horn.

No more the fields with scatter'd grain supply
The restless wand'ring tenants of the STY;
From oak to oak they run with eager haste,
And wrangling share the first delicious taste
Of fallen ACORNS; yet but thinly found
Till the strong gale have shook them to the ground.
It comes; and roaring woods obedient wave:
Their home well pleas'd the joint adventurers leave:
The trudging sow leads forth her numerous young,
Playful, and white, and clean, the briars among,
Till briars and thorns increasing, fence them round,
Where last year's mould'ring leaves bestrew the ground,
And o'er their heads, loud lash'd by furious squalls,
Bright from their cups the rattling treasure falls;
Hot thirsty food; whence doubly sweet and cool
The welcome margin of some rush-grown pool,
The wild duck's lonely haunt, whose jealous eye
Guards every point; who sits prepar'd to fly,
On the calm bosom of her little lake,
Too closely screen'd for ruffian winds to shake;
And as the bold intruders press around,
At once she starts, and rises with a bound:
With bristles rais'd the sudden noise they hear,
And ludicrously wild, and wing'd with fear,
The herd decamp with more than swinish speed,

And snorting dash thro' sedge, and rush, and reed:
Through tangling thickets headlong on they go,
Then stop, and listen for their fancied foe;
The hindmost still the growing panic spreads,
Repeated fright the first alarm succeeds,
Till Folly's wages, wounds and thorns, they reap:
Yet glorying in their fortunate escape,
Their groundless terrors by degrees soon cease,
And Night's dark reign restores their wonted peace.
For now the gale subsides, and from each bough
The roosting pheasant's short but frequent crow
Invites to rest; and huddling side by side,
The herd in closest ambush seek to hide;
Seek some warm slope with shagged moss o'erspread,
Dry'd leaves their copious covering and their bed.
In vain may *Giles*, thro' gath'ring glooms that fall,
And solemn silence, urge his piercing call:
Whole days and nights they tarry midst their store,
Nor quit the woods till oaks can yield no more.

Beyond bleak *Winter's* rage, beyond the *Spring*
That rolling Earth's unvarying course will bring,
Who tills the ground looks on with mental eye,
And sees next *Summer's* sheaves and cloudless sky;
And even now, whilst Nature's beauty dies,
Deposits SEED, and bids new harvests rise;
Seed well prepar'd, and warm'd with glowing lime,
'Gainst earth-bred grubs, and cold, and lapse of time:
For searching frosts and various ills invade,
Whilst wint'ry months depress the springing blade.
The plough moves heavily, and strong the soil,
And clogging harrows with augmented toil
Dive deep: and clinging mixes with the mould
A fat'ning treasure from the nightly fold,
And all the cow-yard's highly valu'd store,
That late bestrew'd the blacken'd surface o'er.
No idling hours are here, when Fancy trims
Her dancing taper over outstretch'd limbs,

And in her thousand thousand colours drest,
Plays round the grassy couch of noontide rest:
Here GILES for hours of indolence atones
With strong exertion, and with weary bones,
And knows no leisure; till the distant chime
Of Sabbath bells he hears at sermon time,
That down the brook sound sweetly in the gale,
Or strike the rising hill, or skim the dale.

Nor his alone the sweets of ease to taste:
Kind rest extends to all;… save one poor beast,
That true to time and pace, is doom'd to plod,
To bring the Pastor to the HOUSE of GOD:
Mean structure; where no bones of heroes lie!
The rude inelegance of poverty
Reigns here alone: else why that roof of straw?
Those narrow windows with the frequent flaw?
O'er whose low cells the dock and mallow spread,
And rampant nettles lift the spiry head,
Whilst from the hollows of the tower on high
The grey-cap'd daws in saucy legions fly.

Round these lone walls assembling neighbours meet,
And tread departed friends beneath their feet;
And new-brier'd graves, that prompt the secret sigh,
Shew each the spot where he himself must lie.
Midst timely greetings village news goes round,
Of crops late shorn, or crops that deck the ground;
Experienc'd ploughmen in the circle join;
While sturdy boys, in feats of strength to shine,
With pride elate their young associates brave
To jump from hollow-sounding grave to grave;
Then close consulting, each his talent lends
To plan fresh sports when tedious service ends.
Hither at times, with cheerfulness of soul,
Sweet *village Maids* from neighbouring hamlets stroll,
That like the light-heel'd does o'er lawns that rove,
Look shyly curious; rip'ning into love;

For love's their errand: hence the tints that glow
On either cheek, an heighten'd lustre know:
When, conscious of their charms, e'en Age looks sly,
And rapture beams from Youth's observant eye.

THE PRIDE of such a party, Nature's pride,
Was lovely POLL;[Footnote: MARY RAYNER, of Ixworth Thorp.]
who innocently
try'd,
With hat of airy shape and ribbons gay,
Love to inspire, and stand in Hymen's way:
But, ere her *twentieth* Summer could expand,
Or youth was render'd happy with her hand,
Her mind's serenity was lost and gone,
Her eye grew languid, and she wept alone;
Yet causeless seem'd her grief; for quick restrain'd,
Mirth follow'd loud, or indignation reign'd:
Whims wild and simple led her from her home,
The heath, the common, or the fields to roam:
Terror and joy alternate rul'd her hours;
Now blithe she sung, and gather'd useless flow'rs;
Now pluck'd a tender twig from every bough,
To whip the hov'ring demons from her brow.
Ill-fated Maid! thy guiding spark is fled,
And lasting wretchedness awaits thy bed …
Thy bed of straw! for mark, where even now
O'er their lost child afflicted parents bow;
Their woe she knows not, but perversely coy,
Inverted customs yield her sullen joy;
Her midnight meals in secresy she takes,
Low mutt'ring to the moon, that rising breaks
Through night's dark gloom:… oh how much more forlorn
Her night, that knows of no returning dawn!…

[Illustration:]

Slow from the threshold, once her infant seat,
O'er the cold earth she crawls to her retreat;

Quitting the cot's warm walls unhous'd to lie,
Or share the swine's impure and narrow sty;
The damp night air her shiv'ring limbs assails;
In dreams she moans, and fancied wrongs bewails.
When morning wakes, none earlier rous'd than she,
When pendent drops fall glitt'ring from the tree;
But nought her rayless melancholy cheers,
Or sooths her breast, or stops her streaming tears.
Her matted locks unornamented flow;
Clasping her knees, and waving to and fro;…
Her head bow'd down, her faded cheek to hide;…
A piteous mourner by the pathway side.
Some tufted molehill through the livelong day
She calls her throne; there weeps her life away:
And oft the gaily passing stranger stays
His well-tim'd step, and takes a silent gaze,
Till sympathetic drops unbidden start,
And pangs quick springing muster round his heart;
And soft he treads with other gazers round,
And fain would catch her sorrow's plaintive sound:
One word alone is all that strikes the ear,
One short, pathetic, simple word,… *"Oh dear!"*
A thousand times repeated to the wind,
That wafts the sigh, but leaves the pang behind!
For ever of the proffer'd parley shy,
She hears the' unwelcome foot advancing nigh;
Nor quite unconscious of her wretched plight,
Gives one sad look, and hurries out of sight….

Fair promis'd sunbeams of terrestrial bliss,
Health's gallant hopes,… and are ye sunk to this?
For in life's road though thorns abundant grow,
There still are joys poor Poll can never know;
Joys which the gay companions of her prime
Sip, as they drift along the stream of time;
At eve to hear beside their tranquil home
The lifted latch, that speaks the lover come:
That love matur'd, next playful on the knee

To press the velvet lip of infancy;
To stay the tottering step, the features trace;…
Inestimable sweets of social peace!

O THOU, who bidst the vernal juices rise!
Thou, on whose blasts autumnal foliage flies!
Let Peace ne'er leave me, nor my heart grow cold,
Whilst life and sanity are mine to hold.

Shorn of their flow'rs that shed th' untreasur'd seed,
The withering pasture, and the fading mead,
Less tempting grown, diminish more and more,
The dairy's pride; sweet Summer's flowing store.
New cares succeed, and gentle duties press,
Where the fire-side, a school of tenderness,
Revives the languid chirp, and warms the blood
Of cold-nipt weaklings of the latter brood,
That from the shell just bursting into day,
Through yard or pond pursue their vent'rous way.

Far weightier cares and wider scenes expand;
What devastation marks the new-sown land!
"From hungry woodland foes go, *Giles*, and guard
The rising wheat; ensure its great reward:
A future sustenance, a Summer's pride,
Demand thy vigilance: then be it try'd:
Exert thy voice, and wield thy shotless gun:
Go, tarry there from morn till setting sun."

Keen blows the blast, or ceaseless rain descends;
The half-stript hedge a sorry shelter lends.
O for a HOVEL, e'er so small or low,
Whose roof, repelling winds and early snow,
Might bring home's comforts fresh before his eyes!
No sooner thought, than see the structure rise,
In some sequester'd nook, embank'd around,

Sods for its walls, and straw in burdens bound:

[Illustration]

Dried fuel hoarded is his richest store,
And circling smoke obscures his little door;
Whence creeping forth, to duty's call he yields,
And strolls the Crusoe of the lonely fields.
On whitethorns tow'ring, and the leafless rose,
A frost-nipt feast in bright vermilion glows:
Where clust'ring sloes in glossy order rise,
He crops the loaded branch; a cumb'rous prize;
And o'er the flame the sputt'ring fruit he rests,
Placing green sods to seat his coming guests;
His guests by promise; playmates young and gay:…
BUT AH! *fresh pastimes* lure their steps away!
He sweeps his hearth, and homeward looks in vain,
Till feeling *Disappointment's* cruel pain,
His fairy revels are exchang'd for rage,
His banquet marr'd, grown dull his hermitage.
The field becomes his prison, till on high
Benighted birds to shades and coverts fly.
Midst air, health, daylight, can he prisoner be?
If fields are prisons, where is Liberty?
Here still she dwells, and here her votaries stroll;
But disappointed hope untunes the soul:
Restraints unfelt whilst hours of rapture flow,
When troubles press, to chains and barriers grow.
Look then from trivial up to greater woes;
From the poor bird-boy with his roasted sloes,
To where the dungeon'd mourner heaves the sigh;
Where not one cheering sun-beam meets his eye.
Though ineffectual pity thine may be,
No wealth, no pow'r, to set the captive free;
Though *only* to thy ravish'd *sight* is given
The golden path that HOWARD trod to heaven;
Thy slights can make the wretched more forlorn,
And deeper drive affliction's barbed thorn.
Say not, "I'll come and cheer thy gloomy cell

With news of dearest friends; how good, how well:
I'll be a joyful herald to thine heart:"
Then fail, and play the worthless trifler's part,
To sip flat pleasures from thy glass's brim,
And waste the precious hour that's due to him.
In mercy spare the base unmanly blow:
Where can he turn, to whom complain of you?
Back to past joys in vain his thoughts may stray;
Trace and retrace the beaten worn-out way,
The rankling injury will pierce his breast,
And curses on thee break his midnight rest.

Bereft of song, and ever cheering green,
The soft endearments of the Summer scene,
New harmony pervades the solemn wood,
Dear to the soul, and healthful to the blood:
For bold exertion follows on the sound
Of distant sportsmen, and the chiding hound;
First heard from kennel bursting, mad with joy,
Where smiling EUSTON boasts her good FITZROY,
Lord of pure alms, and gifts that wide extend;
The farmer's patron, and the poor man's friend:
Whose mansion glitt'ring with the eastern ray,
Whose elevated temple, points the way,
O'er slopes and lawns, the park's extensive pride,
To where the victims of the chace reside,
Ingulf'd in earth, in conscious safety warm,
Till lo! a plot portends their coming harm.

In earliest hours of dark unhooded morn,
Ere yet one rosy cloud bespeaks the dawn,
Whilst far abroad THE FOX pursues his prey,
He's doom'd to risk the perils of the day,
From his strong hold block'd out; perhaps to bleed,
Or owe his life to fortune or to speed.
For now the pack, impatient rushing on,
Range through the darkest coverts one by one;
Trace every spot; whilst down each noble glade

That guides the eye beneath a changeful shade,
The loit'ring sportsman feels th' instinctive flame,
And checks his steed to mark the springing game.
Midst intersecting cuts and winding ways
The huntsman cheers his dogs, and anxious strays
Where every narrow riding, even shorn,
Gives back the echo of his mellow horn:
Till fresh and lightsome, every power untried,
The starting fugitive leaps by his side,
His lifted finger to his ear he plies,
And the view halloo bids a chorus rise
Of dogs quick-mouth'd, and shouts that mingle loud,
As bursting thunder rolls from cloud to cloud.
With ears erect, and chest of vigorous mould,
O'er ditch, o'er fence, unconquerably bold,
The shining courser lengthens every bound,
And his strong foot-locks suck the moisten'd ground,
As from the confines of the wood they pour,
And joyous villages partake the roar.
O'er heath far stretch'd, or down, or valley low.
The stiff-limb'd peasant, glorying in the show,
Pursues in vain; where youth itself soon tires,
Spite of the transports that the chace inspires;
For who unmounted long can charm the eye,
Or hear the music of the leading cry?

Poor faithful TROUNCER! thou canst lead no more;
All thy fatigues and all thy triumphs o'er!
Triumphs of worth, whose honorary fame
Was still to follow true the hunted game;
Beneath enormous oaks, Britannia's boast,
In thick impenetrable coverts lost,
When the warm pack in fault'ring silence stood,
Thine was the note that rous'd the list'ning wood,
Rekindling every joy with tenfold force,
Through all the mazes of the tainted course.
Still foremost thou the dashing stream to cross,
And tempt along the animated horse;

Foremost o'er fen or level mead to pass,
And sweep the show'ring dew-drops from the grass;
Then bright emerging from the mist below
To climb the woodland hill's exulting brow.

Pride of thy race! with worth far less than thine,
Full many human leaders daily shine!
Less faith, less constancy, less gen'rous zeal!…
Then no disgrace mine humble verse shall feel;
Where not one lying line to riches bows,
Or poison'd sentiment from rancour flows;
Nor flowers are strewn around Ambition's car:…
An honest dog's a nobler theme by far.
Each sportsman heard the tidings with a sigh,
When Death's cold touch had stopt his tuneful cry;
And though high deeds, and fair exalted praise,
In memory liv'd, and flow'd in rustic lays,
Short was the strain of monumental woe:
"Foxes, rejoice! here buried lies your foe.[A]"
[Footnote A: Inscribed on a stone in Euston Park wall.]

In safety hous'd, throughout NIGHT'S *length'ning* reign,
The Cock sends forth a loud and piercing strain;
More frequent, as the glooms of midnight flee,
And hours roll round, that brought him liberty,
When Summer's early dawn, mild, clear, and bright,
Chas'd quick away the transitory night:…
Hours now in darkness veil'd; yet loud the scream
Of Geese impatient for the playful stream;
And all the feather'd tribe imprison'd raise
Their morning notes of inharmonious praise;
And many a clamorous Hen and cockrel gay,
When daylight slowly through the fog breaks way,
Fly wantonly abroad: but ah, how soon
The shades of twilight follow hazy noon,
Short'ning the busy day!… day that slides by
Amidst th' unfinish'd toils of HUSBANDRY;
Toils still each morn resum'd with double care,

To meet the icy terrors of the year;
To meet the threats of *Boreas* undismay'd,
And *Winter's* gathering frowns and hoary head.

THEN welcome, COLD; welcome, ye *snowy* nights!
Heaven midst your rage shall mingle pure delights,
And confidence of hope the soul sustain,
While devastation sweeps along the plain:
Nor shall the child of poverty despair,
But bless THE POWER that rules the *changing year;*
Assur'd,… tho' horrors round his cottage reign,…
That *Spring* will come, and Nature smile again.

WINTER.

ARGUMENT.

Tenderness to cattle. Frozen turnips. The cow-yard. Night. The farm-house. Fire-side. Farmer's advice and instruction. Nightly cares of the stable. Dobbin. The post-horse. Sheep-stealing dogs. Walks occasioned thereby. The ghost. Lamb time. Returning Spring. Conclusion.

[Illustration]

WINTER.

IV.

With kindred pleasures mov'd, and cares opprest,
Sharing alike our weariness and rest;
Who lives the daily partner of our hours,
Thro' every change of heat, and frost, and show'rs;
Partakes our cheerful meals, partaking first
In mutual labour and in mutual thirst;
The kindly intercourse will ever prove
A bond of amity and social love.
To more than man this generous warmth extends,
And oft the team and shiv'ring herd befriends;
Tender solicitude the bosom fills,
And Pity executes what Reason wills:
Youth learns compassion's tale from every tongue,
And flies to aid the helpless and the young;

When now, unsparing as the scourge of war,
Blasts follow blasts, and groves dismantled roar,
Around their home the storm-pinch'd CATTLE lows,
No nourishment in frozen pastures grows;
Yet frozen pastures every morn resound
With fair abundance thund'ring to the ground.
For though on hoary twigs no buds peep out,
And e'en the hardy bramble cease to sprout,
Beneath dread WINTER'S level sheets of snow
The sweet nutritious *Turnip* deigns to grow.
Till now imperious want and wide-spread dearth
Bid Labour claim her treasures from the earth.
On GILES, and such as Giles, the labour falls,
To strew the frequent load where hunger calls.
On driving gales sharp hail indignant flies,
And sleet, more irksome still, assails his eyes;
Snow clogs his feet; or if no snow is seen,

The field with all its juicy store to screen,
Deep goes the frost, till every root is found
A rolling mass of ice upon the ground.
No tender ewe can break her nightly fast,
Nor heifer strong begin the cold repast,
Till *Giles* with pond'rous beetle foremost go,
And scatt'ring splinters fly at every blow;
When pressing round him, eager for the prize,
From their mixt breath warm exhalations rise.

If now in beaded rows drops deck the spray,
While *Phoebus* grants a momentary ray,
Let but a cloud's broad shadow intervene,
And stiffen'd into gems the drops are seen;
And down the furrow'd oak's broad southern side
Streams of dissolving rime no longer glide.

THOUGH NIGHT approaching bids for rest prepare,
Still the flail echoes through the frosty air,
Nor stops till deepest shades of darkness come,
Sending at length the weary laborer home.
From him, with bed and nightly food supplied,
Throughout the yard, hous'd round on every side,
Deep-plunging Cows their rustling feast enjoy,
And snatch sweet mouthfuls from the passing boy,
Who moves unseen beneath his trailing load,
Fills the tall racks, and leaves a scatter'd road;
Where oft the swine from ambush warm and dry
Bolt out, and scamper headlong to their sty,
When *Giles* with well-known voice, already there,
Deigns them a portion of his evening care.

Him, though the cold may pierce, and storms molest, Succeeding
hours shall cheer with warmth and rest:

[Illustration]

Gladness to spread, and raise the grateful smile,
He hurls the faggot bursting from the pile,
And many a log and rifted trunk conveys,
To heap the fire, and to extend the blaze
That quiv'ring strong through every opening flies,
Whilst smoaky columns unobstructed rise.
For the rude architect, unknown to fame,
(Nor symmetry nor elegance his aim)
Who spread his floors of solid oak on high,
On beams rough-hewn, from age to age that lie,
Bade his *wide Fabric* unimpair'd sustain
Pomona's store, and cheese, and golden grain;
Bade from its central base, capacious laid,
The well-wrought chimney rear its lofty head;
Where since hath many a savoury ham been stor'd,
And tempests howl'd, and Christmas gambols roar'd.

FLAT on the *hearth* the glowing embers lie,
And flames reflected dance in every eye:
There the long billet, forc'd at last to bend,
While frothing sap gushes at either end,
Throws round its welcome heat:… the ploughman smiles,
And oft the joke runs hard on sheepish *Giles*,
Who sits joint tenant of the corner-stool,
The converse sharing, though in duty's school;
For now attentively 'tis his to hear
Interrogations from the Master's chair.

'LEFT ye your bleating charge, when daylight fled,
'Near where the hay-stack lifts its snowy head?
'Whose fence of bushy furze, so close and warm,
'May stop the slanting bullets of the storm.
'For, hark! it blows; a dark and dismal night:
'Heaven guide the traveller's fearful steps aright!
'Now from the woods, mistrustful and sharp-ey'd,
'The *Fox* in silent darkness seems to glide,
'Stealing around us, list'ning as he goes,
'If chance the Cock or stamm'ring cockerel crows,

'Or Goose, or nodding Duck, should darkling cry,
'As if appriz'd of lurking danger nigh:
'Destruction waits them, *Giles*, if e'er you fail
'To bolt their doors against the driving gale.
'Strew'd you (still mindful of the unshelter'd head)
'Burdens of straw, the cattle's welcome bed?
'Thine heart should feel, what thou may'st hourly see,
'*That duty's basis is humanity.*
'Of pain's unsavoury cup tho' thou may'st taste,
'(The wrath of Winter from the bleak north-east,)
'Thine utmost suff'rings in the coldest day
'A period terminates, and joys repay.
'Perhaps e'en now, while here those joys we boast,
'Full many a bark rides down the neighb'ring coast,
'Where the high northern waves tremendous roar,
'Drove down by blasts from *Norway's* icy shore.
'The *Sea-boy* there, less fortunate than thou,
'Feels all thy pains in all the gusts that blow;
'His freezing hands now drench'd, now dry, by turns;
'Now lost, now seen, the distant light that burns,
'On some tall cliff uprais'd, a flaming guide,
'That throws its friendly radiance o'er the tide.
'His labours cease not with declining day,
'But toils and perils mark his watry way;
'And whilst in peaceful dreams secure *we* lie,
'The ruthless whirlwinds rage along the sky,
'Round his head whistling;… and shall thou repine,
'While this protecting roof still shelters thine?'

Mild, as the vernal show'r, his words prevail,
And aid the moral precept of his tale:
His wond'ring hearers learn, and ever keep
These first ideas of the restless deep;
And, as the opening mind a circuit tries,
Present felicities in value rise.
Increasing pleasures every hour they find,
The warmth more precious, and the shelter kind;
Warmth that long reigning bids the eyelids close,

As through the blood its balmy influence goes,
When the cheer'd heart forgets fatigues and cares,
And drowsiness alone dominion bears.

Sweet then the ploughman's slumbers, hale and young,
When the last topic dies upon his tongue;
Sweet then the bliss his transient dreams inspire,
Till chilblains wake him, or the snapping fire:

He starts, and ever thoughtful of his team,
Along the glitt'ring snow a feeble gleam
Shoots from his lantern, as he yawning goes
To add fresh comforts to their night's repose;
Diffusing fragrance as their food he moves
And pats the jolly sides of those he loves.
Thus full replenish'd, perfect ease possest,
From night till morn alternate food and rest,
No rightful cheer withheld, no sleep debar'd,
Their each day's labour brings its sure reward.
Yet when from plough or lumb'ring cart set free,
They taste awhile the sweets of liberty:
E'en sober *Dobbin* lifts his clumsy heels
And kicks, disdainful of the dirty wheels;
But soon, his frolic ended, yields again
To trudge the road, and wear the clinking chain.

Short-sighted DOBBIN!... thou canst only see
The trivial hardships that *encompass* thee:
Thy chains were freedom, and thy toils repose,
Could the poor *post-horse* tell thee all his woes;
Shew thee his bleeding shoulders, and unfold
The dreadful anguish he endures for gold:
Hir'd at each call of business, lust, or rage,
That prompt the trav'eller on from stage to stage.
Still on *his* strength depends their boasted speed;
For them his limbs grow weak, his bare ribs bleed;
And though he groaning quickens at command,

Their extra shilling in the rider's hand
Becomes his bitter scourge:… 'tis *he* must feel
The double efforts of the lash and steel;
Till when, up hill, the destin'd inn he gains,
And trembling under complicated pains,
Prone from his nostrils, darting on the ground,
His breath emitted floats in clouds around:
Drops chase each other down his chest and sides,
And spatter'd mud his native colour hides:
Thro' his swoln veins the boiling torrent flows,
And every nerve a separate torture knows.
His harness loos'd, he welcomes eager-eyed
The pail's full draught that quivers by his side;
And joys to see the well-known stable door,
As the starv'd mariner the friendly shore.

Ah, well for him if here his suff'rings ceas'd,
And ample hours of rest his pains appeas'd!
But rous'd again, and sternly bade to rise,
And shake refreshing slumber from his eyes,
Ere his exhausted spirits can return,
Or through his frame reviving ardour burn,
Come forth he must, tho' limping, maim'd, and sore;
He hears the whip; the chaise is at the door:…
The collar tightens, and again he feels
His half-heal'd wounds inflam'd; again the wheels
With tiresome sameness in his ears resound,
O'er blinding dust, or miles of flinty ground.
Thus nightly robb'd, and injur'd day by day,
His piece-meal murd'rers wear his life away.

What say'st thou, *Dobbin?* what though hounds await
With open jaws the moment of thy fate,
No better fate attends *his* public race;
His life is misery, and his end disgrace.
Then freely bear thy burden to the mill;
Obey but one short law,… thy driver's will.
Affection, to thy memory ever true,

Shall boast of mighty loads that *Dobbin* drew;
And back to childhood shall the mind with pride
Recount thy gentleness in many a ride
To pond, or field, or village fair, when thou
Held'st high thy braided mane and comely brow;
And oft the Tale shall rise to homely fame
Upon thy gen'rous spirit and thy name.

Though faithful to a proverb, we regard
The midnight chieftain of the farmer's yard,
Beneath whose guardianship all hearts rejoice,
Woke by the echo of his hollow voice;
Yet as the Hound may fault'ring quit the pack,
Snuff the foul scent, and hasten yelping back;
And e'en the docile Pointer know disgrace,
Thwarting the gen'ral instinct of his race;
E'en so the MASTIFF, or the meaner Cur,
At times will from the path of duty err,
(A pattern of fidelity by day;
By night a *murderer*, lurking for his prey);
And round the pastures or the fold will creep,
And, coward-like, attack the peaceful *sheep*:
Alone the wanton mischief he pursues,
Alone in reeking blood his jaws imbrues;
Chasing amain his fright'ned victims round,
Till death in wild confusion strews the ground;
Then wearied out, to kennel sneaks away,
And licks his guilty paws till break of day.

The deed discover'd, and the news once spread,
Vengeance hangs o'er the unknown culprit's head:
And careful *Shepherds* extra hours bestow
In patient *watchings* for the common foe;
A foe most dreaded now, when rest and peace
Should wait the season of the flock's increase.

In part these nightly terrors to dispel,
GILES, ere he sleeps, his little Flock must tell.
From the fire-side with many a shrug he hies,
Glad if the full-orb'd Moon salute his eyes,
And through the unbroken stillness of the night
Shed on his path her beams of cheering light.
With saunt'ring step he climbs the distant stile,
Whilst all around him wears a placid smile;
There views the white-rob'd clouds in clusters driv'n,
And all the glorious pageantry of heav'n.
Low, on the utmost bound'ry of the sight,
The rising vapours catch the silver light;
Thence Fancy measures, as they parting fly,
Which first will throw its shadow on the eye,
Passing the source of light; and thence away,
Succeeded quick by brighter still than they.
For yet above these wafted clouds are seen
(In a remoter sky, still more serene,)
Others, detach'd in ranges through the air,
Spotless as snow, and countless as they're fair;
Scatter'd immensely wide from east to west,
The beauteous 'semblance of a *Flock* at rest.
These, to the raptur'd mind, aloud proclaim
Their MIGHTY SHEPHERD'S everlasting Name.

Whilst thus the loit'rer's utmost stretch of soul
Climbs the still clouds, or passes those that roll,
And loos'd *Imagination* soaring goes
High o'er his home, and all his little woes,
TIME glides away; neglected Duty calls:
At once from plains of light to earth he falls,
And down a narrow lane, well known by day,
With all his speed pursues his sounding way,
In thought still half absorb'd, and chill'd with cold;
When, lo! an object frightful to behold;
A grisly SPECTRE, cloth'd in silver-gray,
Around whose feet the waving shadows play,
Stands in his path!… He stops, and not a breath

Heaves from his heart, that sinks almost to death.
Loud the owl halloos o'er his head unseen;
All else is silent, dismally serene:
Some prompt ejaculation, whisper'd low,
Yet bears him up against the threat'ning foe;
And thus poor Giles, though half inclin'd to fly,
Mutters his doubts, and strains his stedfast eye.
"'Tis not my crimes thou com'st here to reprove;
'No murders stain my soul, no perjur'd love:
'If thou'rt indeed what here thou seem'st to be,
'Thy dreadful mission cannot reach to me.
'By parents taught still to mistrust mine eyes,
'Still to approach each object of surprise
'Lest Fancy's formful visions should deceive
'In moon-light paths, or glooms of falling eve,
'This then's the moment when my heart should try
'To scan thy motionless deformity;
'But oh, the fearful task! yet well I know
'An aged ash, with many a spreading bough,
'(Beneath whose leaves I've found a Summer's bow'r,
'Beneath whose trunk I've weather'd many a show'r,)
'Stands singly down this solitary way,
'But far beyond where now my footsteps stay.
'Tis true, thus far I've come with heedless haste;
'No reck'ning kept, no passing objects trac'd:…
'And can I then have reach'd that very tree?
'Or is its reverend form assum'd by thee?'
The happy thought alleviates his pain:
He creeps another step; then stops again;
Till slowly, as his noiseless feet draw near,
Its perfect lineaments at once appear;
Its crown of shiv'ring ivy whispering peace,
And its white bark that fronts the moon's pale face.
Now, whilst his blood mounts upward, now he knows
The solid gain that from conviction flows;
And strengthen'd Confidence shall hence fulfill
(With conscious Innocence more valued still)
The dreariest task that winter nights can bring,
By church-yard dark, or grove, or fairy ring;

Still buoying up the timid mind of youth,
Till loit'ring Reason hoists the scale of Truth.
With these blest guardians *Giles* his course pursues,
Till numbering his heavy-sided ewes,
Surrounding stillness tranquilize his breast,
And shape the dreams that wait his hours of rest.

As when retreating tempests we behold,
Whose skirts at length the azure sky unfold,
And full of murmurings and mingled wrath,
Slowly unshroud the smiling face of earth,
Bringing the bosom joy: so WINTER flies!…
And see the Source of Life and Light uprise!
A height'ning arch o'er southern hills he bends;
Warm on the cheek the slanting beam descends,
And gives the reeking mead a brighter hue,
And draws the modest *primrose* bud to view.
Yet frosts succeed, and winds impetuous rush,
And hail-storms rattle thro' the budding bush;
And night-fall'n LAMBS require the shepherd's care,
And teeming EWES, that still their burdens bear;
Beneath whose sides tomorrow's dawn may see
The milk-white strangers bow the trembling knee;
At whose first birth the pow'rful instinct's seen
That fills with champions the daisied green:
For ewes that stood aloof with fearful eye,
With stamping foot now men and dogs defy,
And obstinately faithful to their young,
Guard their first steps to join the bleating throng.

But casualties and death from damps and cold
Will still attend the well-conducted fold:
Her tender offspring dead, the dam aloud
Calls, and runs wild amidst the unconscious crowd:
And orphan'd sucklings raise the piteous cry;
No wool to warm them, no defenders nigh.
And must her streaming milk then flow in vain?
Must unregarded innocence complain?

No;… ere this strong solicitude subside,
Maternal fondness may be fresh apply'd,
And the adopted stripling still may find
A parent most assiduously kind.
For this he's doom'd awhile disguis'd to range,
(For fraud or force must work the wish'd-for change;)
For this his predecessor's skin he wears,
Till cheated into tenderness and cares,
The unsuspecting dam, contented grown,
Cherish and guard the fondling as her own.

Thus all by turns to fair perfection rise;
Thus twins are parted to increase their size:
Thus instinct yields as interest points the way,
Till the bright flock, augmenting every day,
On sunny hills and vales of springing flow'rs
With ceaseless clamour greet the vernal hours.

The humbler *Shepherd* here with joy beholds
The approv'd economy of crowded folds,
And, in his small contracted round of cares,
Adjusts the practice of each hint he hears:
For Boys with emulation learn to glow,
And boast their pastures, and their healthful show
Of well-grown Lambs, the glory of the Spring;
And field to field in competition bring.

E'en GILES, for all his cares and watchings past,
And all his contests with the wintry blast,
Claims a full share of that sweet praise bestow'd
By gazing neighbours, when along the road,
Or village green, his curly-coated throng
Suspends the chorus of the spinner's song;
When Admiration's unaffected grace
Lisps from the tongue, and beams in every face:
Delightful moments!… Sunshine, Health, and Joy,
Play round, and cheer the elevated Boy!

'*Another* SPRING!' his heart exulting cries;
'*Another* YEAR! with promis'd blessings rise!…
'ETERNAL POWER! from whom those blessings flow,
'Teach me still more to wonder, more to know:
'*Seed-time* and *Harvest* let me see again;
'Wander the *leaf-strewn* wood, *frozen* plain:
'Let the first Flower, corn-waving Field, Plain, Tree,
'Here round my home, still lift my soul to THEE;
'And let me ever, midst thy bounties, raise
'An humble note of thankfulness and praise!' —

APRIL 22, 1798.

NOTES

A fav'rite morsel with the Rook, &c. P. 9, l. 104.

In these verses, which have much of picturesque, there is a severe charge against *Rooks and Crows*, as very formidable depredators; and their destruction, as such, seems to be recommended. Such was the prevalent opinion some years back. It is less general now: and I am sure the humanity of the Author, and his benevolence to Animals in general, will dispose him to rejoice in whatever plea can be offered in stay of execution of this sentence. And yet more so, if it shall appear that ROOKS, at least, deserve not only mercy, but *protection* and *encouragement* from the Farmer.

I shall quote a passage from BEWICK'S interesting HISTORY of BIRDS: the narrative part of which is often as full of information as the embellishments cut in wood are beautiful…. It is this.

Speaking of Birds of the PIE-KIND in general, he says "Birds of this kind [Footnote: P. 63] are found in every part of the known world, from Greenland to the Cape of Good Hope. In many respects they may be said to be of singular benefit to mankind: principally by destroying great quantities of noxious insects, worms, and reptiles. ROOKS, in particular, are fond of the erucae of the *hedge-chaffer*, or chesnut *brown beetle*: for which they search with indefatigable pains. These insects," he adds in a note, "appear in hot weather in formidable numbers: disrobing the fields and trees of their verdure, blossoms, and fruit; spreading desolation and destruction wherever they go…. They appeared in great numbers in IRELAND during a hot summer, and committed great ravages. In the year 1747 whole meadows and corn-fields were destroyed by them in SUFFOLK. The decrease of Rookeries in that County was thought to be the occasion of it. The many Rookeries with us is in some measure the reason why we have so few of these destructive animals."[Footnote: Wallis's History of Northumberland.]

"Rooks," he subjoins, "are often accus'd of feeding on the corn just after it has been sown, and various contrivances have been made both to kill and frighten them away; but, in our estimation, the advantages deriv'd from the destruction which they make among grubs, earth-worms, and noxious insects of various kinds, will greatly overpay the injury done to the future harvest by the small quantity of corn they may destroy in searching after their favourite food." [Footnote: Mr. Bewick does not seem to have been quite aware that much of this mischief, as I have been informed by a sensible neighboring Farmer and Tenant, is done in the grub-state of the chaffer by biting through the *roots* of grass, &c. A latent, and imperceptibly, but rapidly spreading mischief, against which the *rooks* and birds of similar instinct are, in a manner, the sole protection. C. L.]

"In general they are sagacious, active, and faithful to each other. They live in pairs; and their mutual attachment is constant. They are a clamorous race: mostly build in trees, and form a kind of society in which there appears something like a regular government. A Centinel watches for the general safety, and gives notice on the appearance of danger."

Under the Title, "ROOKS," (p. 71) Mr. BEWICK repeats his observations on the useful property of this Bird.

I confess myself solicitous for their safety and kind treatment. We have two which were lam'd by being blown down in a storm (a calamity which destroys great numbers almost every spring). One of them is perfectly domesticated. The other is yet more remarkable; since although enjoying his natural liberty completely, he recognizes, even in his flights at a distance from the house, his adoptive home, his human friends, and early protectors.

The ROOK is certainly a very beautiful and very sensible Bird; very confiding, and very much attach'd. It will give me a pleasure, in which I doubt not that the Author of this delightful Poem will partake, if any thing here said shall avail them with the Farmer; and especially with the SUFFOLK FARMER.

C. L.

Destroys life's intercourse; the social plan. P. 46, l. 341.

"Allowing for the imperfect state of sublunary happiness, which is comparative at best, there are not, perhaps, many nations existing whose situation is so desirable; where the means of subsistence are so easy, and the wants of the people so few. The evident distinction of ranks, which subsists at *Otaheite*, does not so materially affect the felicity of the nation as we might have supposed. The simplicity of their whole life contributes to soften the appearance of distinctions, and to reduce them to a level. Where the climate and the custom of the country do not absolutely require a perfec: garment; where it is easy at every step to gather as many plants as form not only a decent, but likewise a customary covering; and where all the necessaries of life are within the reach of every individual, at the expence of a trifling labour; ambition and envy must in a great measure be unknown. It is true, the highest classes of people possess some dainty articles, such as pork, fish, fowl, and cloth, almost exclusively; but the desire of indulging the appetite in a few trifling luxuries can at most render individuals, and not whole nations, unhappy. Absolute want occasions the miseries of the lower class in some civiliz'd states, and is the result of the unbounded voluptuousness of their superiors. At *Otaheite* there is not, in general, that disparity between the highest and the meanest man, that subsists in England between a reputable tradesman and a labourer. The affection of the Otaheitans for their chiefs, which they never fail'd to express upon all occasions, gave us great reason to suppose that they consider themselves as one family, and respect their eldest borm in the persons of their chiefs. The lowest man in the nation speaks as freely with his king as with his equal, and has the pleasure of seeing him as often as he likes. The king, at times, amuses himself with the occupations of his subjects; and not yet deprav'd by false notions of empty state, he often paddles his own canoe, without considering such an employment derogatory to his dignity. How long such an happy equality may last is uncertain: and how much the introduction of foreign luxuries may hasten its dissolution cannot be too frequently repeated to Europeans. If the knowledge of a few individuals can only be acquired at such a price as the happiness of nations, it were better for the discoverers and the discovered that the *South Sea* had still remain'd unknown to *Europe* and its restless inhabitants."

REFLECTIONS ON OTAHEITE: Cook's second Voyage.

APPENDIX

When the FIRST EDITION of this POEM appear'd in March last, I intimated a design of accompanying it with some CEITICAL RE-MARKS. With that design various Engagements have since greatly interfer'd. From one of the most laborious and constant of those, that of the office of a Justice of the Peace for the County of Suffolk, I am now discharg'd. Why those who are in power have done this, they have not explain'd: and it being an office from which any one who holds it is removable at *pleasure*, they are not call'd to explain. Had it been for Crime or Misconduct as a Magistrate, of course Trial and Conviction should have preceded my Removal. As it is, I feel, as I have publicly declar'd, no shame in the removal. I have held an office honorable because extensively useful; because unprofitable and burthensome to the individual; because independently and conscientiously exercis'd, with a devotion, such as it requir'd, of my time, my thoughts, and my best faculties, daily to its discharge. My Collegues,—and they are and have been, during a course of seventeen years, those of them who now act, and those who are dead or absent, men with whom to have acted was indeed satisfactory and pleasant,—my late Collegues part with me, and I with them, regrettingly. Our reciprocal Esteem is not lessen'd by this abruption of our official intercourse. And as every man who feels what Society is, ought to determine to be serviceable to the Public, my removal from this office neither weakens the determination, nor probably will be found to have impair'd the means of effecting it. I am therefore well content;—as I ought to be. I sought not the office. I have never sought any. It solicited my acceptance; unask'd and unexpected. I owe my appointment to the Duke of GRAFTON, very soon after I came to reside in this County. He was then *Lord Lieutenant.* I have not yielded that appointment to disgust; though there were those who were not sparing in their endeavours to disgust me with it: I have not relinquished it to suit my convenience; though in times like these an office of no little expence, and which shut me out from sources of professional emolument, was to me certainly not convenient: I have not consulted my ease or health by a voluntary retirement. I am remov'd, I am superseded, I am struck out from an office of incredible and hourly increasing anxiety. Circumstances like this are not new. They have repeatedly taken place in relation to very high offices; and the Public remembers men to whom they have happen'd whose internal dignity and worth is above any official dignity. Had I felt that I *merited* to be remov'd, I should not have thought myself a fit Editor of the FARMER'S BOY; a Poem which breathes every where modest independence, benevolence, innocence, and virtue. As it is, I think myself no way less fit than ever for any laudable and becoming employ. And I have accordingly announc'd my intention of resuming my profession as a BARRISTER. In the mean time, the leisure which has thus been thrown to me may properly and usefully be devoted to the Remarks which I had before meditated; and for which I had in some measure pledg'd myself to the PUBLIC.

The FIRST of these will naturally be that which relates to the *manner* and circumstances of the Composition. There is such proof in it of Genius disregarding difficulty, and of powers of retention and arrangement, that it will be believ'd I could not overpass it: and that it would have been stated at the first if it had been then in my power to state it.

I now lay it before the Public in the words of Mr. SWAN: who in a Letter address'd to me in *The Ladies Museum* of this Month, after congratulating me on my "successful efforts," (and with such a Production to propose to public Attention how could they be unsuccessful?) "in rescuing from oblivion a Poem, which for the harmony of its numbers, the beauty of its imagery, originality of thought, elegance and chasteness of diction, (every circumstance consider'd,) stands unrivall'd in the Annals of English Literature, and will descend to Posterity with increasing celebrity," states the *motive* on which he writes: (a motive well meriting a Letter and a public statement:) "to throw light upon the manner of the composition of the Farmer's Boy; which appears to him (and most justly) no inconsiderable addition to the well-earn'd laurels of the Author."

For the pleasure of the view which it includes of the character and manners of Mr. BLOOMFIELD, I shall, with the Author of this interesting Letter, go beyond the mere fact; and give his narration of the cause and manner of the *Discovery*, as well at the Discovery itself.

Mr. SWAN thus expresses himself:

"From the pleasure I receiv'd in reading the FARMER'S BOY, and from some strange coincidences in the early part of Mr. Bloomfield's life with my own, I was naturally enough anxious to become acquainted with the Author. For this purpose I obtain'd his address, and found him ... the modest, the unambitious person you describe; wondering at the praise and admiration with which his Poem has been receiv'd; whose utmost ambition was to have presented a fair copy to his aged Mother, as a pledge of filial affection, and a picture of his juvenile avocations. So unexpected was the fame of his production, that the whole of his good fortune appears to him as a dream." — 'I had no more idea,' says he, 'to be sent for by the Duke of Grafton, and be so kindly and generously treated, than of the hour I shall die.'

"I gave him," Mr. SWAN continues, "my card of address, an invitation to my house, and a sincere profession of friendship; if, among his numerous admirers, and noble and royal patrons, the latter was worthy of acceptance."

"Last Sunday afternoon [Footnote: The Letter is dated 12 July, 1800.] I was highly pleas'd with his company, and gratified and entertain'd with his conversation. — Sir, he is all ... nay, more than you have describ'd."

"Among other subjects of conversation respecting the *Farmer's Boy*, I wish'd to be inform'd of his manner of composition. I enquir'd, as he compos'd it in a garret, amid the bustle and noise of six or seven fellow workmen, whether he us'd a slate; or wrote it on paper with a pencil, or pen and ink. But what was my surprize when told that he had us'd neither. — My business, during the greatest part of my life having led me into the line of litterary pursuits, and made me acquainted with litterary men, I am, consequently, pretty well inform'd of the methods us'd by authors for the retention of their productions. We are told, if my recollection is just, that Milton took his Daughters as his amanuenses; that Savage, when his poverty precluded him the conveniency of pen, ink, and paper, us'd to study in the streets, and go into shops to record the productions of his fertile genius; that Pope, when on visits at Lord Bolingbroke's, us'd to ring up the servants at any hour in the night for pen and ink, to write any thought that struck his lively and wakeful imagination; that Dr. Blacklock, though blind, had the happy faculty of writing down, in a very legible hand, the chaste and elegant productions of his Muse."

"With these and many other methods of composition we are acquainted; but that of a great part of *the Farmer's Boy* stands, in my opinion, first on the List of Litterary [Footnote: I have ventur'd to restore litterary to that mode of spelling, with the double *t*, which the Analogy of our language seems to require. L.] Phaenomena.—Sir, Mr. Bloomfield, either from the contracted state of his pecuniary resources to purchase Paper, or from other reasons, compos'd the latter part of his *Autumn* and the whole of his *Winter* in his head, without committing one line to paper.—This cannot fail to surprize the Litterary World: who are well acquainted with the treacherousness of memory, and how soon the most happy ideas, for want of sufficient quickness in noting down, are lost in the rapidity of thought."

"But this is not all.—He went still a step farther.—He not only compos'd and committed that part of the work to his retentive memory, but he corrected it all in his head. And, as he said, when it was thus prepar'd,… *I had nothing to do but to write it down.*"

"By this new and wonderful mode of composition he studied and completed his Farmer's Boy in a garret; among six or seven workmen, without their ever suspecting any thing of the matter."

"Sir, this to me was both new and wonderful: and induc'd me rather to communicate the information to you through the medium of the Press than by writing; that it may meet the eye of many, who will be equally struck and pleas'd with the novelty of the idea as myself."

I have on this part of the subject, only, after quoting thus much at present from the Letter of Mr. SWAN, to add, that I entirely agree with him, I believe, as to the force, clearness, and comprehensiveness of intellect manifested by this experiment, and its success.

I now pass to part of what has been fully and excellently said by Dr. DRAKE of HADLEIGH, while investigating the merits of this astonishing
Rural Poem.

In a Letter from HADLEIGH [Footnote: 9 March, 1800.] Dr. DRAKE had given me this distinct and vivid representation of his general idea of the Poem.

"I have read THE FARMER'S BOY with a mixture of astonishment and delight. There is a pathetic simplicity in his sentiments and descriptions that does honour to his head and heart."

"His copies from Nature are truly original and faithful, and are touched with the hand of a Master.... His versification occasionally displays an energy and harmony which might decorate even the pages of a DARWIN."

"The general characteristics of his Style, however, are sweetness and ease. In short, I have no hesitation in declaring, that I think it, as a Rural and descriptive Poem, superior to any production since the days of
THOMSON."

"It wants no reference to its Author's uneducated poverty to render its excellence the more striking; they are such as would confer durable Fame on the first and most polish'd Poet in the Kingdom."

I shall now take the liberty of extracting part of the CRITIQUE which Dr. DRAKE, agreeably to his intimation to me, has made of the FARMER'S BOY in his LITTERARY HOURS.[Footnote: Vol. II, Ess. xxxix, p. 444.]

"From the pleasing duty of describing such a 'character' (meaning the personal character of Mr. BLOOMFIELD) let us now turn our attention to the species of composition of which his Poem is so perfect a specimen. It has been observ'd in my sixteenth number that PASTORAL POETRY in this country, with very few exceptions, has exhibited a tame and servile adherence to classical imagery and costume; at the same time totally overlooking that profusion of picturesque beauty, and that originality of manner and peculiarity of employment, which our climate and our rustics every where present."

"A few Authors were mention'd in that Essay as having judiciously deviated from the customary plan: to these may now be added the name of *Boomfield*; the *Farmers Boy*, though not assuming the form of an Eclogue, being peculiarly and exclusively, throughout, a *pastoral Composition*; not like the Poem of *Thomson*, taking a wide excursion through all the phenomena of the *Seasons*, but nearly limited to the rural *occupation* and business of the fields, the dairy, and the farm yard."

"As with these employments, however, the vicissitudes of the Year are immediately and necessarily connected, Mr. Bloomfield has, with propriety, divided his Poem into *Four* Books, affixing to those Books the Titles of the Seasons."

"Such indeed are the merits of this Work, that in true *pastoral* imagery and simplicity I do not think any production can be put in competition with it since the days of Theocritus." [Footnote: I have heard that the opinion of no less a Judge than Dr. WATSON, Bishop of LLANDAFF, is by no means short of the encomium implied in this comparison, high and ample as it is. L.]

"To that charming simplicity which particularizes the Grecian, are added the individuality, [Footnote: Much of these qualities indeed is certainly in *Theocritus* also. L.] fidelity, and boldness of description, which render Thomson so interesting to the lovers of Nature."

"GESNER possesses the most engaging sentiment, and the most refin'd simplicity of manners; but he wants that rustic wildness and naïveté in delineation characteristic of the Sicilian, and of the composition before us."

"WARNER and DRAYTON have much to recommend them: but they are very unequal; and are devoid of the *sweet and pensive morality* which pervade almost every page of *the Farmers Boy*; nor can they establish any pretensions to that fecundity in painting the oeconomy of rural life, which this Poem, drawn from actual experience, so richly displays."

"It is astonishing indeed what various and striking circumstances, peculiar to the occupation of the *British Farmer*, and which are adapted to all the purposes of the *pastoral* Muse, had escaped our Poets, previous to the publication of Mr. *Bloomfield's* Work."

"Those who are partial to the *Country;*—and where is the man of Genius who feels not a delight approaching to ecstasy from the contemplation of its scenery, and the happiness which its cultivation diffuses?—those who have paid attention to the process of husbandry, and who view its occurrences with interest; who are at the same time alive to all the minutiae of the animal and vegetable creation; who mark

'How Nature paints for colours, how the Bee
Sits on the bloom, extracting liquid sweet,'

will derive from the study of this Poem a gratification the most permanent and pure."

Though I have thus largely extracted I cannot omit transferring
hither the
ANALYSIS of the Poem, as given by Dr. Drake.

"The *first* Book, intitled *Spring,* opens with an appropriate invocation. A transition is then made to the artless character of *Giles,* the *Farmer's Boy;* after which the scene near *Euston* in Suffolk is describ'd, and an amiable portrait of Mr. *Austin,* immediately follows.

"Seed-time, harrowing, the devastation of the rooks,[Footnote: I will not say much: but I was glad to see since the second Edition of this Poem the cause of the Rooks had again been advocated, in the *Newcastle Chronicle.* L.] wood-scenery, the melody of birds, cows milking, and the operations of the dairy, occupy the chief part of this Season: which is clos'd by a beautiful Personification of the Spring and her attendants, and an admirable delineation of the sportive pleasures of the young Lambs."

"The *second* Book, or *Summer,* commences with a characteristic sketch of the prudent yet benevolent Farmer. The genial influence of the rain is then welcom'd; to which succeeds a most delicious picture of a green and woody covert with all its insect tribe. The ascension of the sky-lark, the peaceful repose of *Giles,* a view of the ripening harvest, with some moral reflections on Nature and her great

Creator, are introduc'd: follow'd by animated descriptions of reaping, gleaning, the honest exultation of the Farmer, the beauty of the Country Girl, and the wholesome refreshment of the field. Animals teazed by insects, the cruelty of docking horses, the insolence of the gander, the apathy of the swine, are drawn in a striking manner: and the Book concludes with masterly pictures of a twilight repose, a midnight storm of thunder and lightning, and views of the ancient and present mode of celebrating Harvest-home."

"The *third* Book, *Autumn*, is introduc'd with a delineation of forest scenery, and pigs fattening on fallen acorns. Sketches of wild ducks and their haunts, of hogs settling to repose in a wood, and of wheat sowing, succeed. The sound of village bells suggests a most pleasing digression: of which the church and its pastor, the rustic amusements of a Sunday, the Village Maids, and a most pathetic description of a distracted Female, are the prominent features. Returning to rural business, *Giles* is drawn guarding the rising wheat from birds: — his little hut, with his preparation for the reception of his playmates, their treachery and his disappointment, are conceiv'd and colour'd in an exquisite style. Fox-hunting, the Fox-hound's epitaph, the long autumnal evenings, a description of domestic fowl, and a welcome to the snowy nights of Winter, form the concluding topics of this Season."

"The *fourth* Book, under the appellation of *Winter*, is usher'd in by some humane injunctions for the treatment of storm-pinch'd cattle. The frozen turnips are broken for them: and the cowyard at night is describ'd. The conviviality of a Christmas evening, and the conversation round the fire, with the admonitions from the Master's chair, are depicted in a manner truly pleasing. The *Sea Boy* and the *Farmers Boy* are contrasted with much effect: and the ploughman feeding his horses at night, with the comparison between the cart-horse and post-horse, have great merit. The mastiff turn'd sheep-biter is next delineated; succeeded by a description of a moon-light night, and the appearance of a spectre."

"The counting of the Sheep in the fold, and the adopted Lambs, are beautiful paintings: and with the Triumph of GILES on the conclusion of the Year, and his Address to the DEITY, the Book and Poem close."

"Such are the Materials of which THE FARMER'S BOY is constructed. Several of the topics, it will be perceiv'd, are new to Poetry; and of those which are in their *title* familiar to the readers of our descriptive Bards, it will be found that the imagery and adjunctive circumstances are original, and the effort of a mind practis'd in the rare art of selecting and combining the most striking and picturesque features of an object."

Dr. Drake after this well accounts for the poetic singularity that the Poetry of *Thomson* should have past through a mind so enthusiastically enamor'd of it, without impairing the originality of its character, when exercis'd on a subject so much leading to imitation. This he explains, and justly, by the vivid impressions on a most sensible and powerful imagination in his earliest youth, anterior to the study of any Poet.

Dr. Drake expresses his astonishment at the VERSIFICATION and DICTION of this Poem. And says most truly, "I am well aware that smooth and flowing lines are of easy purchase, and the property of almost every poetaster of the day: but the versification of Mr. *Bloomfield* is of another character; it displays beauties of the most positive kind, and those witcheries of expression which are only to be acquir'd by the united efforts of Genius and Study."

"The *general* characteristics of his versification are facility and sweetness; that ease which is, in fact, the result of unremitted labour, and one of the most valuable acquisitions of litterature. It displays occasionally likewise a vigour and a brilliancy of polish that might endure comparison with the high-wrought texture of the Muse of DARWIN. From the nature of his subject, however, this splendid mode of decoration could be us'd but with a sparing hand: and it is not one of his least merits that his diction and harmony should so admirably correspond with the scene which he has chosen."

"To excel," Dr. DRAKE continues, "in rural IMAGERY, it is necessary that the Poet should diligently study Nature for himself; and not peruse her as is but too common, '*through the spectacles of Books*' [Footnote: The happy illustration of DRYDEN in his admirable character of SHAKESPERE.] He should trace her in all her windings, in her deepest recesses, in all her varied forms. It was thus that

LUCRETIUS and VIRGIL, that THOMSON and COWPER were enabled to unfold their scenery with such distinctness and truth: and on this plan, while wandering through his native fields, attentive to '*each rural sight, each rural sound,*' has Mr. BLOOMFIELD built his charming Poem."

"It is a Work which proves how inexhaustible the features of the World we inhabit: how from objects which the mass of mankind is daily accustom'd to pass with indifference and neglect. GENIUS can still produce pictures the most fascinating, and of the most interesting tendency. For it is not to *imagery* alone, though such as here depicted might ensure the meed of Fame, that the Farmer's Boy will owe its value with us and with posterity. A *Morality* the most *pathetic* and pure, the feelings of a heart alive to all the tenderest duties of humanity and religion, consecrate its glowing landscapes, and shed an interest over them, a spirit of devotion, that calm and rational delight which the goodness and greatness of the Creator ought ever to inspire."

Dr. DRAKE confirms, by copious and very judicious *Extracts* from the various parts of the Poem, as they offer themselves to critical selection, in accompanying the Farmer's Boy through the Circle of his year, the Judgment which he has form'd with so much ability, taste, and feeling, and has to agreeably express'd, of the Merits of our ENGLISH GEORGIC. And he speaks in his *third* and last Essay on it thus:

"From the review we have now taken of THE FARMER'S BOY, it will be evident, I think, that owing to its harmony and sweetness of versification, its benevolence of sentiment, and originality of imagery, it is entitled to rank very high in the class of descriptive and *pastoral* Poetry."

He concludes with an highly animated and feeling anticipation of that public attention to the Poem and to its Author, merited in every view, and which already has manifested itself in such an extent.

I understand there is a Paper on "*The Farmer's Boy*" in a Work lately publish'd by Dr. ANDERSON; and assuredly from its subject well entitled to attention, as well as from the abilities and public spirit of its Editor;—AGRICULTURAL RECREATIONS. Where indeed with more appropriate Honor could such a Poem be notic'd?

In the *Critical Remarks* I intended I find myself so much agreeing in sentiment with Dr. Drake that I shall attempt little more than merely to offer some few observations. One of these relates to the *coincidences* of thought and manner in the Farmer's Boy with other writings. These, as would previously be expected from what has been said, are extremely few indeed. And almost all that are particularly of moment in appreciating the poetical excellences of the Work are most truly *coincidences*, and cannot be otherwise consider'd.

For the first of these which I shall mention I am indebted to WILLIAM SMITH, Esq. of BURY, who had largely his share of Public Admiration, when he sustain'd for many years with great skill and judgment, and great natural advantages, almost every character of our Drama which had been eminently favor'd by either Muse; and who now enjoys retirement with honor and merited esteem.

He mention'd to me in conversation, and since by Letter, a passage very closely resembling one in the IDYLLIA of AUSONIUS. It is this in *Spring*.

Like the torn flower the fair assemblage fly.
Ah, fallen *Rose*! sad emblem of their doom;
Frail as thyself, *they perish while they bloom*! I.v. 388-40.

The passage to which Mr. Smith referr'd me is this. (It is not in my Edition of *Ausonius*; but he sent me a Copy.)

"Conquerimur, Natura, brevis quod Gratia florum est;
   Ostentara oculis illico dona rapis.
 Quam longa una dies aetas tarn longa rosarum,
   Ques *pubescentes juncta senecta pressit*."

ID. xiv.

I am favor'd with a Translation made by Mr. SMITH in his very early days.
And hope that as a brother *Etonian* he allows me to quote it.

Nature, we grieve that thou giv'st flowers so gay,
Then snatchest Gifts thou shew'st so swift away.
A Day's a Rose's Life. — *How quickly meet,*
Sweet Flower, thy Blossom and thy Winding sheet!

In the *Procession* of SPRING there is a fine series of allegorical
Images.

Advancing SPRING profusely spreads abroad
Flowers of kinds, with sweetest fragrance stor'd:
  Where she treads LOVE gladdens every plain;
Delight on tip-toe beats her lucid train;
  Sweet *Hope* with conscious brow *before* her flies,
  Anticipating wealth from summer skies.

  I. v. 271—6.

  Compare now this of LUCRETIUS.

It VER et VENUS et Veneris *praenuntius ante*
Prunatus *graditur* Zephyrus vestigia propter.
FLORA quibus mater praespergens, ante viai
Cuncta coloribus egregiis et odoribus opplet.

DE NAT. RES. L. V. v. 736-9.
Ed. Brindley 1749.

There SPRING, and VENUS, and her Harbinger,
Near to her moves the winged Zephyrus,
For whom maternal FLORA strews the way
With Flowers of every charming scent and hue.

  Or in the very words of BLOOMFIELD,

  Flowers of all hues with sweetest fragrance stor'd.

Hope here occupies the place of *Zephyrus.* DELIGHT on tip-toe
supporting the *lucid* train of *Spring,* — the image and attitude so full

of life and beauty,—is our Poet's own. And what Poet, what *Painter*, would not have been proud of it?

In another passage,

The splendid raiment of the Spring peeps forth
Her universal Green—

This of Lucretius will be found to have much similitude:

Camposque per omnes
Florida fulserunt viridami prata colore.

782, 3.

O'er every plain The flowery meadows beam with verdant hue.

And that exceedingly fine verse,

All Nature feels her venorating sway,

calls to mind the ever-memorable exordium of the *Roman* Poet.

If we admire the imitative force of this line in the epic majesty of Virgilian numbers,

Quadrupedante putrem sonitu qualit ungula campum:

Shakes the resounding hoof the trembling plain:

shall we not admire the imitative harmony of this; attun'd certainly with not less felicity to the sweetness of the pastoral reed,

The green turf trembling as they bound along.

The pause on the first syllable of the verse has been an admir'd beauty in
Homer and Milton.

[Greek: Nux ech d'espchsen enchos.] II.

And over them triumphant Death his dart
Shook, but delay'd to strike. P.L.

We have this beauty,—coinciding with the best examples, though underiv'd from them,—in a cadence of most pathetic softness.

Joys which the gay companions of her prime
Sip, as they drift along the stream of time.

III. v. 169, 70.

The beautiful Description of the Swine and Pigs feeding on fallen Acorns reminds me of a most picturesque one, not now at hand, in GILPIN on *Forest Scenery.*

The turn of this thought,

Say not, I'll come and cheer thy gloomy cell.

III. v. 241, &c.

I believe is from Scripture. Prov. iii. 28. And so I think certainly is that,

'Till Folly's wages, wounds and thorns, they reap.

III. 37.

But the most remarkable of all, and where I had no expectation of finding a similitude, is in near the close of the *Winter.*

Far yet above these wafted clouds are seen
(In a remoter sky yet more serene)
Others, detach'd in ranges through the air,
Spotless as snow, and countless as they're fair;
Scatter'd immensely wide from east to west,
The beauteous semblance of a Flock at rest.

IV. 255—60.

In HERCULES the LION-SLAYER there is this passage:

…….. Tad epaeluthe piona maela,
Ech soianaes anionia mei aulia ie saechsie,
Ayiar epeiia soes, mala muriai, akkai ep allais
Erchomenai phainonth, osei NEPHE HYDATOENTA
'Hossat' en thrano eisi elaunomena prolepose
Aee Noloioio ziae ae Thraekos Boreao.
Ton meni thlis arithmos en aeeri ginei ionion,
Oui anusis lisa gar ie meia proloioi chulindei
Is anemth, iade i alla chorusselai authis ep allois
Toss aiei melopisthe zoon epi zthcholi aeei.
Pan dar eneplaesthae pedion, pasaile cheleuthai,
Aaeidos erchomenaes.

HAERAKL. LEONTOPH.

Idyll. Theocrito adscriptum. Brunckii Analect. I. 360.

…….. On came the comely sheep,
From feed returning to their pens and fold.
And these the *Kine*, in multitudes, succeed;
One on the other rising to the eye;
As watery CLOUDS which in the Heavens are seen,
Driven by the south or Thracian *Boreas*,
And, numberless, along the sky they glide:
Nor cease; so many doth the powerful Blast
Speed foremost, and so many, fleece on fleece,
Successive rise, reflecting varied light
So still the herds of Kine successive drew
A far extended line: and fill'd the plain,
And all the pathways, with the coming troop.

* * * * *

I may possibly enlarge these Remarks in a future Edition. At present I am happy to be stopt here, by so good a cause as the urgency of the Publishers to complete a Third Edition; they informing me that the second is entirely out of print. But it is pleasant to see these Coincidences with CLASSIC POETS of other days and Nations in a CLASSIC of our own, of the best School:

"The fields his study, Nature was his book."

C.L.

TROSTON, 22 Aug. 1800.

THE END.